FRANCIS and CLARE,
Saints of Assisi

FRANCIS and CLARE,
Saints of Assisi

by HELEN WALKER HOMAN
illustrations by John Lawn

VISION BOOKS
Farrar, Straus & Cudahy   New York
Burns & Oates   London

MANUFACTURED IN THE UNITED STATES OF AMERICA
PUBLISHED SIMULTANEOUSLY IN CANADA BY AMBASSADOR
BOOKS, LTD., TORONTO

To my Board of Editors:

JONATHAN, ANTHONY, GEOFFREY,
and
WILLIAM GREENE

Nihil Obstat:

> Rt. Rev. Msgr. Peter B. O'Connor
> *Censor Librorum*

Imprimatur:

> ✠ Most Reverend Thomas A. Boland, S.T.D.
> *Archbishop of Newark*

The nihil obstat and imprimatur are official declarations that a book or pamphlet is free of doctrinal or moral error. No implication is contained therein that those who have granted the nihil obstat and imprimatur agree with the contents, opinions or statements expressed.

Author's Note

THE story of Francis and Clare, the Saints of Assisi, as retold for boys and girls in the following pages, adheres to the established dates, facts, and events. Where legend mingles with history, the two have been blended to give emphasis to the personalities of the subjects, about whom has clung for seven centuries a perpetual perfume of devotion rising from the hearts of the faithful.

Because the records of the childhood of each are scanty, some scenes and minor characters have been invented in order to round out what we know is true about these saints. In the later portion of the book, events follow the accepted record; but again, as in the introductory portion, some of the dialogue has been invented to give point to traditional history.

For source material, the author is indebted to some long and happy visits in Assisi, and to the rich field of Franciscan history and legend. From the early sources: *The Lives of St. Francis of Assisi*, by Brother Thomas of Celano; *The Legend of St. Francis*, by the Three Companions; *The Life of St. Francis*, by St. Bonaventura; *The Mirror of Perfection*, by Friar Leo;

The Little Flowers of St. Francis; and other early manuscripts.

The modern sources include among others: *Life of St. Francis of Assisi,* by Paul Sabatier (Scribner's, 1930); *St. Francis of Assisi,* by G. K. Chesterton (Doubleday, 1944); and *St. Francis of Assisi,* by Omer Englebert (Burns & Oates, 1950).

Contents

	Author's Note	9
I	The House with a Dungeon	13
II	The Dragon on the Ring	33
III	The Tavern of The Three Angels	53
IV	The Prisoner of Perugia	77
V	The Last Feast	87
VI	The Search for the Face	99
VII	The Fairest Lady of Them All	111
VIII	The Beggar and His Little Portion	129
IX	The Door of the Dead	143
X	The Sultan and His Golden Tent	159
XI	The Dawn of Holy Cross Day	173
XII	The Song at Sunset	185
	And After . . .	189

ONE

The House with a Dungeon

THE Lady Pica flung open the casement and called down to the boy in the garden. As she leaned out, her long blue veil, the color of the Italian sky, blew across the deep window ledge and floated like a banner against the gray stone wall.

It was a fair garden she looked down upon that spring morning of the year 1189, bright with blossoming fruit trees and flowers, green with lawn and vegetables. Beyond it, one could see the ancient walls of Assisi with

their high turrets which protected the city from its
enemies; and beyond these, the soft, limitless sky.

"If you are coming to market with me, Francis, it is
time to make ready, for Maria and I will be leaving
very soon," the Lady Pica said.

The boy, crouched before a little wicker cage on
the ground, looked up and smiled.

"I come, *Mamma Mia*," he called, as he held a bit
of lettuce beneath the quivering nose of a small brown
hare inside the cage. "Look, for the first time he is
eating a good breakfast! He is getting well."

"Good. Now hurry, dear, or all the nice things will
be gone," replied his mother as she closed the casement.

Francis, who was seven, gave a last gentle touch to
the hare's bandaged leg. It was healing nicely, he
thought. That had been a cruel thing. He had found
the small creature high up on the hillside more than a
week ago, hiding in a cave, with its leg dangling limply.
Probably it had been chased by one of the fierce dogs
which roamed the mountain and had somehow hurt its
leg. With soft words, Francis had picked it up gently
and had carried it home under his cloak.

For a year now, he had kept the wicker cage in the
garden for just such events. The small hospital was
almost never empty. Sometimes the patient was a bird
which had fallen from a nest, or again a stray puppy
which had suffered from bad company. When the creature was healed, Francis would open the door wide and
say:

"Now go back into the world, my friend; but next time, learn to be more careful!"

On this spring morning, the birds were singing messages to each other back and forth between the leafy trees, and as he ran up the path toward the house, Francis could hear laughter coming from the street. The world seemed so happy, and he heard his own heart singing right along with the birds. Dashing through the low arch which led to the kitchen, he almost fell over his brother Angelo who was seated on a bench, carving out something from a piece of wood.

"Clumsy!" cried Angelo. "Watch where you're going. Can't you see I'm carving?"

Angelo was four years older than Francis.

"Oh, it's a dagger!" exclaimed Francis breathlessly, leaning over his brother's shoulder. His big brown eyes sparkled with pleasure. "It's very fine indeed!"

"Not nearly so fine as the *real* dagger which our father said he would bring me from France," replied Angelo. "I'm old enough to have one now," he added proudly, "but you're not."

"Stuff!" exclaimed Maria, the housekeeper, who was stirring a pot over the fire.

She was a middle-aged widow, stout and strong, and she had a daughter, Lucia, who helped her in the house.

"You're still not old enough to behave like a man in the kitchen," went on Maria to Angelo. "See all those shavings you have left on the floor. And look at the peelings from that plum you have just eaten! Pick them up now, at once, before your lady mother sees them!"

But Angelo went right on with his carving. His small brother stood at his side, looking on with admiration, and twisting his foot this way and that with every move that Angelo made.

"I suppose," said the older one scornfully, "that *you* are going with the women to market."

Francis nodded.

"Well, while you're tagging after the women, like the baby you are, I shall be having my lesson in fencing."

"I'm not a baby!" protested Francis hotly. "And I go with our lady mother to the market only to protect her and Maria."

Angelo threw back his head and laughed loudly.

"Protect!" he cried. "You are a fine protector, with those skinny arms and legs. And from whom, pray, do you protect them?"

"From the brigands," answered Francis seriously.

"Brigands!" roared Angelo, bent double with laughter.

"Well," said Francis, turning red and twisting the other foot, "every one says there are brigands about."

"Not in broad daylight, you goose. And not in the market place with all those people. They hide way up on the mountain and come out only at night."

He got up from the bench and looked at the dagger with satisfaction.

"This will serve until our father brings me one of steel from France," he said.

Striding out to the middle of the floor, he stuck the weapon in his belt, and with one hand upon it, swaggered back and forth, his short cloak swinging from his shoulder.

"I shall wear it like this, as do the knights," he said. "And this is how I shall use it!"

He grasped the dagger by the hilt and, throwing one leg behind him, began striking at an imaginary enemy.

"See, this is the way to attack," he said. "A quick eye —and one must be very fast on one's feet."

He began dancing back and forth; and, as Angelo was rather fat, he looked very funny. Just then he slipped on the plum skins he had dropped on the floor. Out went his feet from under him, and the dagger flew from his hand. Swiftly Francis picked it up, and before the surprised Angelo could rise, the younger boy was dancing and strutting about the kitchen, imitating his brother.

"Here's Angelo!" he cried, his small face drawn into a fierce frown.

Maria stopped stirring the pot to shriek with laughter, for the imitation that Francis was giving of his big brother was indeed comic.

"That young one is like a monkey," she gasped between her shrill laughs. "He can mimic anyone to perfection, from the *podesta* down."

Now the *podesta* was the mayor of Assisi, and a very important person. He had a red beard and wore about his neck a big golden chain which jangled loudly as he went about the town, putting everyone in his place.

But Angelo, stretched out on the floor, was not laughing. Anger clouded his face as he got up slowly and made for Francis.

"Give me back my dagger!" he cried, lunging toward his small brother.

But Francis dodged quickly, and then sped into the large chamber which opened off the kitchen, with Angelo in hot pursuit. He caught up with his brother on the wide stairway which led to the upper rooms, and just then the Lady Pica started down the stairs. All that she could see of her two sons was a wild scramble of legs and arms.

"Stop that at once!" she cried firmly.

Angelo slowly let go of Francis and, frowning, got to his feet.

"He took my dagger and then made fun of me."

"Francis, give that dagger back at once and pick yourself up. A fine sight you are now to enter the market place with us! Go to Maria and let her fix your clothes. And be sure to wash your face and hands."

Now one of the strange things about the Bernardone house was an opening in the stone wall at the back. It was much shorter than a closet, so that even a boy, if he were tall, could not stand upright in it. Instead of a door, it had a gate of strong bars and a huge lock with a great brass key. It was here that Pietro Bernardone, the boys' father, put any of his servants who had been dishonest —locking them up until he could bring them before the *podesta* to be judged. While they waited, the prisoners could only sit on the cold stone floor with their knees bent double, and reach out eagerly between the bars for the food and water which Maria brought them. It was a most uncomfortable spot. In the great palaces of Assisi, such places were deep underground and were called dungeons.

So now Angelo turned to his mother and said:

"Francis should be put in the little dungeon for what he did!"

"Nonsense," she replied sternly. "If anyone is to be punished, it should be you for beating your little brother. Now stop frowning and be off and get ready for your fencing lesson."

Francis, sore from the thumping he had received, made off for the kitchen, feeling very thankful indeed that his mother had come along just when she did.

When he had finished washing, and when Maria had taken a stitch in his hose, torn in the scuffle, the Lady Pica came and stood in the arched doorway. Her blue veil was held in place by a tiny golden crown and floated down over her shoulders. "Her eyes are quite as blue as her veil and she looks just like the Madonna; she is very beautiful, my mother," thought Francis, smiling at her. Maria now took down her brown mantle from a peg on the wall and picked up her market basket.

"Come along," smiled the Lady Pica, holding out her hand to Francis.

The three left the house by the great front door, and, just as they were leaving the fencing master arrived.

"By the time you return, baby," Angelo called after Francis, "I shall be as fine a swordsman as any knight in Umbria!" For Assisi lies in that part of Italy which is known as Umbria. Francis retorted with a gay smile and made a comic face at his brother.

Under the bright sun of this lovely morning, the city gleamed like a jeweled crown on its hillside crest. The house faced a pleasant street where brightly colored flowers grew in pots on the wide window ledges and spilled themselves down against the soft gray walls. As they started out, the Lady Pica looked back at her home with pleasure. She loved this house to which Pietro Bernardone had brought her as a bride. Apart from the great palaces of the nobles, it was one of the finest in Assisi; and so it should be. For the Lady Pica herself was of noble birth and her husband was the richest merchant in town. From him, the nobles bought all their fine silks and velvets.

In those days, not only the great ladies, but also the lords, were dressed in rich materials and gay colors. And there was no one in all Assisi who could provide these but Bernardone, the merchant. To get them, he had to travel great distances over the mountains into France and into Spain where the finest silks and satins were made. With a large company of servants and horses, he would be gone for months, buying the beautiful things he would bring home to sell in his shop in Assisi. At this very moment, Pietro Bernardone was off on just such a journey to France.

As they went toward the market, the Lady Pica and

Francis walked first, and behind them came Maria with her basket. Just down the street from the house stood the Church of San Giorgio, and, next to it, the school where Angelo and Francis learned their Latin and took lessons in writing. Francis looked at the school and said to his mother:

"When will school begin again, *Mamma Mia?*"

"Why, not until fall when the cool weather comes," she replied. "The good priests cannot be expected to teach during the hot summer."

"I hope it will be a long time until the fall," sighed Francis. "I don't like school."

"Your father will be sorry to hear this when he returns. You know he wishes you to learn and to grow up to be wise and brave so that some day you may become a great knight."

"I'd like to be a knight but I don't want to study," said Francis.

"But you cannot be a knight unless you do. And don't forget that your French master is coming this afternoon. Your father especially wants you to speak French, so you must listen very carefully as Master Jacques teaches you."

"I like French well enough," said Francis, "but I don't care much for Master Jacques."

"I'm surprised," said his mother. "Being French, he can teach you well; and we must all be very kind to him, for he is far from his native land which he dearly loves."

"Well, I wish he would go back there," said Francis.

Francis was eager to reach the market place which was always full of people, all talking at once and laughing as they moved about buying what they wanted and arguing loudly over the price. There were animals there, too—horses and donkeys tied to the posts, and dogs and cats running about looking for scraps of food. His mother always gave him a few coins with which to buy bread for the beggars who stood about the square holding out their hands. Francis felt very sorry for them. They had nothing but rags to wear, and they looked very thin and hungry. His mother also gave him money to buy grain for the pigeons.

Now he ran up the hill ahead of the others. Today the market place was gayer and more crowded than he had ever seen it. Piled high everywhere were the goods the country people were selling. Besides all the people who had come to buy, there was a company of knights who had just ridden into the square. The long plumes of their helmets danced in the breeze, and each had a sword and a dagger at his side. Their horses were covered with rich trappings.

"It is a company from Perugia," explained a friend to the Lady Pica. "They have ridden over to attend the wedding feast of the Lord Montessori. Let us praise heaven that Assisi and Perugia are now at peace so we need have no fear of battle."

"Indeed, yes," exclaimed the other. "There has been far too much blood spilled between the youth of the two cities. Now, thank God, they can mingle as friends."

The city of Perugia lay only a few hours' ride away from Assisi. It, too, was built on a hillside, with high walls set all about it. In those days, in Italy, city made war upon city, even as countries do today. Assisi and Perugia were ancient enemies and, to tell the truth, the *podesta* was none too happy about these visitors today, even though the two cities were at peace. A careless word at the feast, and a little too much wine, and steel might clash against steel.

Francis ran joyfully in and out of the crowd to get closer to the knights. He wanted to look at each one carefully, and at their horses, so that he could make up his mind now just how he, himself, would look when he grew up. He most admired the fair knight who wore pale blue velvet and silver, and who gave him a kindly smile as Francis patted his horse and looked up at him in wonder. He became so excited that he almost forgot the bread for the beggars. But at last he found his mother again, and he could see that Maria's basket was now quite full. The Lady Pica took some coins from the red leather purse which hung from a golden chain at her waist, and Francis found a man who was selling bread.

"I want the biggest loaf you have," he said, proudly holding out his money.

"Now run along to your beggars," smiled his mother. "I shall be waiting for you on the bench where we always sit."

Off flew Francis with the loaf and soon was dividing it among his poor friends who every day waited for him.

"God bless you, Master Francis!" they called after him as he went to join his mother.

"And God bless you, too, my friends," he called back over his shoulder.

Stopping a moment to buy some grain for the pigeons, he found the Lady Pica seated on a stone bench at the very edge of the square. It was on the side overlooking the great plain which stretched out into the far distance below Assisi. Maria, with her heavy basket, had already started for home. Francis leaned against the balustrade and gazed out over the miles of open country spreading below. It was very beautiful, he thought. The good God had made such a big world! And here and there on the plain, He had planted clumps of green trees, tall and slender, and had spilled the streams which curved in and out among them like silver ribbons.

"Your pigeons are waiting," called his mother.

Francis turned to see a flock of them clustered at her feet, pushing each other this way and that. He sat down on the bench and began to toss out the grain, laughing with delight at the tricks the puffy birds played to outwit each other in pecking up the seeds.

"It was just such a lovely day as this when you were born," said the Lady Pica, looking up at the tall mountain which rose above them. "The Mount of Subasio was covered with wild flowers and the look of spring, and everywhere the birds were singing. Your father was away in France. When he returned, he insisted that you should be named Francis because of his great love

for that land. Now you see why you must do well with
your French and learn to speak it as you do your own
tongue."

Just then they heard happy shouts and looked up to
see a crowd of children dancing about a man and a
woman who were dressed very strangely. The man wore
a long red stocking, reaching up to his waist, on one
leg, and on the other, a bright green one with patches
of yellow silk shaped like diamonds. On his head was
a cap with a long point which fell over his nose, and
from it little bells jingled merrily. Over her face the
woman wore a mask which looked like a bird's head
with a long beak; and her tight orange dress trailed off
at the back into a long tail of feathers. They were really
actors, but in those days they were called *jongleurs*.

"The *jongleurs*, the *jongleurs!*" shouted Francis,
jumping to his feet and clapping his hands.

Now the two strange figures came up to the Lady
Pica and bowed low before her.

"Would you like to see our play, fair lady?" asked
the man.

"Oh, please, *Mamma Mia!*" cried Francis.

His mother smiled and nodded. Francis curled up
beside her and the other children sat at her feet while
the players began to act out a very funny play about a
man trying to catch a bird. Every now and then they
would stop to sing a song and then to dance. The Lady
Pica and all the children laughed and clapped; and at
the end, the Lady Pica opened her purse and threw some

coins to the actors. With many bows, and calling out
their thanks, the *jongleurs* moved away, the crowd of
children following after. Francis gave his mother a hug
to thank her and then said:

"When I grow up, *Mamma Mia,* I shall also be a
jongleur!"

"A *jongleur?*" she asked in surprise. "But I thought
you were going to be a knight. Now you can't be both
a knight and a *jongleur!*"

Suddenly Francis became very sad. He sat thinking
for a moment and then began to smile again.

"But I could be a *jongleur* first, *Mamma Mia;* and
then later I could be a knight!"

"No," said the Lady Pica, "that would not be possible,
for one has to begin very early the training for knight-
hood."

She got up from the bench. "Come, we must hurry,
for we have yet to stop at your father's shop; and we
must not be late for your lesson."

The shop of Pietro Bernardone lay close to his home.
To Francis it always seemed the most wonderful place
in the world. Across it stretched a long counter of oak
on which were laid out great rolls of shimmering silk
and velvet. But Francis liked best of all the bright cloth
of gold such as was worn only by princes. It would
be very nice to be a prince, he thought, and to wear
cloth of gold.

His father's man, Roberto, greeted them.

"Welcome, my Lady and Master Francis," he said.

"I have been hoping that you would come today, for already there have been many in and out, asking when the master will return."

"I feel sure, Roberto, that he is now on his way home and that almost any day you will see the company ride up," answered the Lady Pica.

"I hope so," sighed Roberto. "Count Roland of Chiusi has been here again today, as he has been every day for the past month, pestering me about the tapestry he ordered especially. And the Lady Leonori has been almost as bad, asking about that roll of sea-green satin she wanted the master to bring from Paris."

Francis, who had been examining the materials spread out on the counter, pointed now to a piece of pale green silk.

"Why don't you sell her that one?" he asked.

Both his mother and Roberto laughed.

"That is not sea-green, dear," she said, "nor is it satin. Wait until you see the ocean, and then you will know how lovely is the color we call sea-green. When you are older, you will come to help your father in the shop; and then Roberto will teach you how to know satin from taffeta."

"But how shall I be able to help my father in the shop if I'm going to be a *jongleur* and then a knight?" asked Francis anxiously.

"Only a knight," she corrected him gently. "But there will be time, too, for you to work in the shop when your father needs you."

When they reached home, Maria said that Master Jacques was waiting outside on the terrace which overlooked the garden. Francis went out to join him.

"Angelo has gone off with his friends for a picnic on the mountain," explained Maria, in the kitchen, to the Lady Pica. "And here is the chicken you asked me to cook for the good priests of San Giorgio."

"Thank you, Maria." Then the Lady Pica went to the door which opened onto the terrace.

"I shall be gone for an hour," she called to Francis. "Work well at your lesson until I return."

As the Lady Pica started off for the church, Maria wiped her hands and took her sewing box down from the shelf. This was the hour she always spent under the fruit trees at the far end of the garden, mending the boys' clothing. She gave a last look at the meal, which was slowly cooking over the big fireplace, and went out through the arch. As she passed the terrace, she could not help smiling at what she saw. Master Jacques was striding up and down, loudly speaking strange words which Maria could not understand. Francis was trying to repeat the words after him. Master Jacques was tall, with a long, thin face and small dark eyes, but with a big nose which turned up at the end. While Maria did not understand the French words, Francis did; and he was not liking his lesson a bit.

"Now repeat this," his teacher was saying. "Everything in France is more beautiful than it is in Italy."

Francis dutifully repeated the words.

"In France, the sky is much more blue," said Master Jacques.

Francis knew this was not true, for he had heard his father say that nowhere was there a bluer sky than in Italy. But frowning, he repeated the words in a low voice.

"French ladies are more lovely than Italian ladies," declared the teacher.

Francis knew that this, also, was not true. For who in the world could be more lovely than his lady mother? But, almost choking, he got the words out somehow.

"And the men in France," went on Master Jacques, "are much braver."

That, too, is a lie, thought Francis. What man lived who was braver than his father? Twice a year he risked his life in long journeys over the Alps, fighting off brigands and thieves who fell upon his caravan at night, and, with drawn knives, tried to kill him.

Suddenly the terrace seemed to have grown very warm. Francis got up and said to his teacher:

"It is much too hot out here to learn French. Let us go on with the lesson in the house."

Master Jacques agreed and followed him into the kitchen. On their way to the large chamber, they passed the little dungeon in the wall.

"What is that?" asked Master Jacques curiously, peering down at it.

"It is a dungeon," explained Francis proudly, "where my father locks up his servants who do not behave well."

"You call that thing a *dungeon?*" Master Jacques threw back his head and laughed very loud. "You should go to France where we have *real* dungeons. The dungeons in France are much larger. Why, this thing isn't big enough to hold a child!"

"Oh, but it is," said Francis, turning the big brass key and opening the gate. "Go inside and try, and you will see for yourself. If you sit down and pull your knees up, you will find that it is quite large enough."

"You are a silly boy," said Master Jacques. "Here, I will show you."

And, still laughing, he bent way down and crawled in. But he was no sooner inside, hunched up like a huge rabbit, than Francis pulled the gate shut and turned the brass key in the lock. Then, putting his face close to the bars, he cried out in French to the surprised teacher:

"The dungeons in France are much larger!"

Then he turned and ran like the wind, out through the kitchen and into the garden. As he ran, he could hear Master Jacques pounding on the bars and crying out in French strange words that he had never taught Francis. Onward the boy sped, down the path toward the wicker cage where his friend, the brown hare, was waiting for him. But suddenly he stopped. He had just remembered that now there was no one in the house at all except the French teacher locked up in the little dungeon and that it would be a long time before anyone returned to let him out.

"Did you know," he asked the brown hare aloud in French, "that the dungeons in France are much larger?"

Then he dropped down on the grass and rolled over several times in a fit of laughter and pounded the earth in his merriment.

TWO

The Dragon on the Ring

EIGHT years had passed and Francis was now fifteen. On his birthday, his father had given him a fine black horse which he had bought from a famous knight in Perugia. Francis called the horse Raphael, the name of the great Angel of Joy; and when Raphael went fast, it truly seemed that he flew on the wings of an angel. Francis himself took care of Raphael and did not like anyone else to touch him.

Now on these mornings, Francis helped his father and Angelo in the shop. In the afternoons, he rode to the palace of a nobleman, a friend of his father, who was teaching him how to ride and to handle his horse like a knight.

One day in September when he had just ridden home after such a lesson, the Lady Pica came out into the courtyard to meet him, carrying a jug wrapped in a napkin.

"My son," she said, "before you dismount I want you to ride to the castle of the Sciffi family and take this jug to the Lady Ortolana. Her little one, Clare, is ill of a fever and this will surely cool it."

Francis bent over the mixture and made a face.

"Why, *Mamma Mia*," he said, laughing, "this is that terrible stuff you used to give us when we were sick. Have you no pity for the little Lady Clare? She's only three and cannot defend herself!"

"Hush, now," replied his mother, "and do as I say. Terrible it may be to the taste, but you remember how it always made you well again."

"I'm only teasing you," Francis answered as he stooped down and took up the jug. "But you had better take my dagger, as it will only be in the way. I shall have to keep Raphael to a walk, or we shall spill all this poison before we reach the castle of the Sciffi!"

"Shall I take your lute, also?" asked his mother.

For Francis had a fine lute tied by a broad blue ribbon about his neck. His father had brought it to him from France.

"No," said Francis, slinging the lute around to his

back, "for perhaps the Lady Ortolana may come to the window and ask me to sing, as she did the last time."

"If she does, be sure to sing that new serenade which the troubadours just taught you," said his mother. "Your father is much pleased with it."

"I shall. And as I sing the French words, I shall try to think kindly of Master Jacques," Francis replied with a wink.

"Indeed you should! For while it was long ago that you locked him up in the little dungeon, I doubt if he has ever forgiven you. I am sure it was *that* which sent him back to France!"

Francis laughed.

"If he knew how sore I was from the beating my father gave me when he returned, he must surely have forgiven me by now," he said.

Giving Raphael a gentle kick, he turned outward through the gate, with the reins in one hand and the jug held under his other arm. His mother watched him as he rode away and thought how grownup he looked. "He rides just as well as he dances," she thought, "for this son of mine is light and full of grace—the grace of body. May the dear God fill his soul equally with grace!"

She was always proud to send him on an errand to the Lady Ortolana. The Sciffi family lived in a great castle with many servants. Certainly her boy's manners were good and he had no cause to be ashamed of his clothing, for his father insisted that it should be made from the finest materials in the shop. No son of the nobility in all Assisi—or in Perugia, either, for that matter—was handsomer or better dressed, thought the Lady Pica.

Francis rode quietly along, humming the song which he hoped to sing to the Lady Ortolana, and he tried to remember just how it was that the troubadours had sung it. Only a few nights before, Pietro Bernardone had asked two troubadours, who were passing through Assisi on their way to Rome, to come and sing for his dinner guests. They had sung a new French ballad which had delighted every one and, later, they had taught it to Francis.

The troubadours were very like the *jongleurs*—except that they sang better and played the lute as they sang— and they did not do comic tricks as did the *jongleurs*. Nor did one find them on the streets or in the market square. They were men who came from a great distance far across the Alps and traveled from castle to castle to sing to the lords and their ladies. Sometimes they would stay for weeks in one castle. They sang songs of war and of brave knights and fair ladies. But of all the songs which the troubadours sang, Francis loved best those about the great King Arthur and his Knights of the Round Table. How he wished that he, himself, could have been one of King Arthur's knights!

He would love to kill the giants and the wicked kings; he would be so happy if only he could rescue a princess from a cruel dragon. But there seemed to be no giants about any more; nor any dragons either, thought Francis sadly. Still, there were many fair ladies and brave knights. There were, too, the great Crusades to the Holy Land; and almost always there were battles going on somewhere. In the past, his own city had often been attacked, and people kept saying that Perugia was not to be trusted—that any day she might strike again. If she did, he might have a chance to prove how brave he could be!

"When that day comes," he said aloud to Raphael, "we shall go forth together—you and I—and do many great deeds for Assisi, for there is no knight anywhere who owns a finer horse than mine!"

Raphael threw up his head and snorted in agreement.

Now they had come to the place where the path turned off to the castle. Francis saw it gleaming through the trees, a great pile of gray stone with the sun warm upon it. From its tower there floated a red and green banner with the coat of arms of the Sciffi family woven in gold upon it. When Francis rode into the courtyard, a servant came forward to meet him. Francis handed him the jug and asked him to take it to the Lady Ortolana. It was for the little Lady Clare, he explained, and he would wait to hear how she was feeling today.

"Perhaps," whispered Francis to Raphael as he patted his neck, "the Lady Ortolana will not ask us to sing at all. Just because she did the last time does not mean that she will today. That would be a good joke on us."

But even as he spoke, a casement above his head flew

open and there stood the Lady Ortolana herself, her dark eyes smiling a welcome.

"Have you a new song to sing to me, Francis?" she called down to him.

Francis was off his horse in an instant, bowing low, his green velvet cap in his hand.

"Indeed, my lady, I have a new song and I shall be honored if you care to hear it. But first, may I ask, how does the little Lady Clare today?"

"She is better, although the fever is still burning her. But I'm sure that the brew which your kind mother has sent will cure her."

"When we were small," said Francis, "it always cured us; but it does have a horrible taste!"

"All children think that medicine has a horrible taste," laughed the Lady Ortolana. "But I shall put some honey with it and the baby will be quite happy to take it. And now, while it is being heated, please let me hear your song."

So Francis lifted the lute from his neck and began to strum the song the troubadours had taught him. It was a song of love, and as he sang, he put all his heart into it, thinking that some day, just so, he would be singing it to the fair lady whom he would ask to be his bride. He would stand beneath her window, just as he now stood beneath the window of the Lady Ortolana. Only then it would be at night, and a big round moon would be glowing like gold in the sky. The more he thought about this, the better he sang the French words which

Master Jacques had taught him long ago. At the end, as he again bowed low, the Lady Ortolana leaned out and dropped a ring at his feet. She smiled and clapped.

"You sing like an angel!" she said. "You must come some evening and dine with us and sing for my lord. Keep the ring as a token of the friendship of the Sciffi family."

Francis stooped and picked it up. It was of gold, carved to look like the head of a dragon, and the dragon held a bright red ruby in its mouth.

"Oh, my lady, it is far too fine for me!" cried Francis.

"Nonsense. Not so many years from now you will be a knight and must wear it in battle. If you are fighting for truth and justice, it will bring you luck."

Francis thanked her gratefully.

"I hope the Lady Clare will soon be well again," he said as he mounted Raphael. "And I shall be glad to come and sing for you and the Lord Faverone whenever it may please you."

Then he and his horse were off at a gallop, with Francis waving a gay farewell.

While he had been gone, his mother and father had been sitting on the terrace at home, watching the sun as it set over the Umbrian plain. Pietro Bernardone was handsome and had flashing dark eyes and a thick black beard. He had been telling his wife of his plans for their sons.

"Angelo will become a merchant, like me," he said, "but Francis is like you and should take his place among the nobility. That is why I am having him trained to be a knight, and taught to speak French, to sing, and to play the lute, for he must marry a noble lady."

The Lady Pica sighed. "I would much rather that he became a good Christian," she said.

Just then Francis himself appeared, flushed and happy.

"The baby is better, and the Lady Ortolana sent you all her thanks, *Mamma Mia*," he cried as he dismounted. "I sang for her—the new song that my father likes." He bowed to his father. "And, at the end, see what she gave me!"

He took the ring from his finger and held it out to his mother.

"It's very beautiful," she said, "but I don't like the dragon. I have heard that dragons bring bad luck."

"Oh, no; this one brings very *good* luck," said Francis.

"But I wonder whether you should accept so fine a gift."

"It was given to me in token of the friendship of the Sciffi," explained Francis.

"In that case," said his mother, "you could not refuse it."

Her husband smiled broadly and gave his wife a look that said: "You see? Things are turning out as I planned." He picked up the ring and examined it closely. "This is a costly jewel," he said. "Be sure, now, that you do not lose it, or allow some one to steal it in those careless moments of yours!"

"Oh, no, my father! I shall keep it always, for I want always to keep the friendship of the Sciffi!

"And there's more to tell you," laughed Francis happily. "The Lady Ortolana has asked me to dine at the castle so that the Lord Faverone may also hear me sing."

Pietro Bernardone beamed. Indeed, things were working out exactly as he had planned. Francis was making his friends among the nobility.

Now, with the hot weather almost past, the priests of San Giorgio had opened their school again, but Francis had won a promise from his father that he need not return. In those days, not many boys continued to go to school after they were fifteen.

Early one morning his father said to him:

"You are to ride over to the fair at Spoleto today where some English merchants are showing their wools. Buy what you think we can sell and bring it back to the shop before evening."

Francis was delighted to have this chance for a long ride with Raphael and to attend the fair. There would be much to see, and undoubtedly there would be many *jongleurs* about from whom he might learn a song, or a trick or two. So, with his purse full of money, he and Raphael gaily set out.

They had to ride past the school, and, although it was early, four or five boys were already there, waiting for the doors to open. They were playing a game of ball

while they waited, and Francis stopped Raphael at the
side of the road to watch them. He was a little sorry
that he felt too grownup to join them, for they all
seemed to be having a very good time. There was one
of them, a tall boy with a kind face, who looked almost
as old as Francis. "I wonder who he is," thought Francis.
"I've never seen *him* before."

Just then, the ball went flying over Raphael's head
and the tall boy ran to catch it. As he leaped into the air,
his feet came down on the edge of a deep ditch at the
side of the road and he lost his balance and tumbled in.
Francis was off Raphael's back in a second and had run
to help him.

"It's only my ankle," said the boy, who could not
stand up. "I must have twisted it again."

"Here, let me help you," said Francis.

With the boy's arm about his shoulder, he managed
to get him out of the ditch and sat him down on a rock.
His companions gathered around. They could see that
their friend's ankle was badly swollen.

"The priests will know how to fix it," said one.

"But how shall I ever get home?" asked the boy. "It's
more than an hour's walk; and even if they bind it up,
I fear I shall not be able to stand on it for some time."

Francis could see that the boy was suffering and
bearing the pain bravely.

"Where do you live?" he asked.

"About four miles away, on the road to Spoleto."

"Why," said Francis, "I'm riding to Spoleto myself,
and you can ride behind me and hold on to my belt."

At that moment the school doors opened. One of the boys soon brought a priest who carried a jar of ointment and a strip of linen.

"My poor Leo," he said kindly, as he skilfully bound the ankle, "you should be more careful. You know that this has happened before. Now you will have to miss a few days of school."

"Oh, I shall make up for it, Father," answered Leo quietly, looking up at him with steady gray eyes. "Thank you for helping me," he added with a smile.

"I never worry about you and your studies," answered the priest, patting him on the shoulder. "Now if you will go home and stay off your feet, I think you will soon be all right again. And a lucky thing it is that young Bernardone rode along just then and will carry you safely home."

Raphael stood quietly while they hoisted Leo up behind Francis. The horse seemed to know what was expected of him, for he walked along gently so as not to jar Leo.

"It's strange that I have never seen you before," said Francis.

"Well, I haven't been in Assisi much," confessed Leo. "I started school only this fall."

"Why was that?" asked Francis.

"We live on a farm," explained Leo, "and my father has to work very hard and has needed my help. But he is so good, my father, that now he has permitted me to enter school."

"So you really wanted to go to school? I'm afraid, had

I been in your shoes, that I should have been only too glad of an excuse to stay away!" laughed Francis.

"My father knows a little Latin," explained the other, "and was teaching me at home in the evenings. But then we got to the place where he did not know any more. Since I liked it and also wanted to learn to write, he said that if I did not mind walking to town every day, I could ask the priests to teach me."

"You have no horse, then?"

"Only one for the farm, and he is always needed there. I'm glad to walk—that is, when I have two ankles to walk with," laughed Leo.

"My father is good, too," said Francis. "He is a merchant, and just now I am riding to the fair to buy things for him. It will be great fun at the fair. I wish you could come with me!"

"Oh, I wish I could!" exclaimed Leo. "If only I had not twisted my ankle!"

"I'll tell you what," said Francis. "The next time I go to Spoleto, I will stop for you at the farm, and we'll make a day of it!"

"I should like that very much," smiled Leo. "Will you then become a merchant, like your father?"

"Oh, no. I'm being trained to be a knight, and I hope some day to follow the Crusaders into battle. And you? Do you plan to be a farmer?" asked Francis.

"I—I can't say yet." Leo was stammering a little. "I have something in mind, but perhaps it is impossible."

He fell silent. Francis somehow knew that Leo felt

sad and that he must not ask him any more questions, so Francis said:

"Perhaps you would like to hear a French song?"

Before the other could answer, he broke into a merry tune, interrupting it every now and then with a loud, comical whistle which made Leo laugh so much that he almost fell off the horse. Even Raphael seemed to enjoy it, for he began to prance a little. By the time they had reached the farm and Leo's father was lifting his son down, the two boys were good friends.

"Come back soon!" called Leo, as Francis started off.

"I will," promised the other, as he waved his cap and set off at a canter down the road.

When he returned to Assisi that evening, the great bell of San Rufino, the cathedral where all the children were baptized, was ringing out the Angelus, and the sky was pink with the afterglow of sunset. Francis had enjoyed a fine day, and his father was well pleased with the wool he had brought back from the fair.

The Bernardone family had scarcely finished its evening meal when there was a knocking at the front door. Maria opened it and admitted a youth who wore on his sleeve the coat of arms of the Sciffi. The messenger carried a letter for Francis; he waited in the hall for an answer. Francis opened it and read aloud:

"The Lord Faverone and the Lady Ortolana bid Francis Bernardone to the birthday feast of their nephew, Orlando, tomorrow evening after sundown. They would be pleased if he would bring his lute."

Although Maria was waiting to take the answer, Francis ran out himself to tell the messenger that he would be pleased to come. When he returned, his father was smiling and his mother was saying: "He must wear the new yellow silken hose and the doublet of green velvet."

But Angelo frowned and said:

"I have seen that young Orlando about the town and he is a wild one, as are all his friends. Sciffi, or no, he is forever in trouble with the *podesta*. Were I in your place, Father, I should not permit Francis to attend this feast."

But no one paid any attention to him, and Francis said:

"Be sure, *Mamma Mia*, to remind me to wear the ring which the Lady Ortolana gave me."

"Yes," said his mother, "and you must not forget either to inquire about the little Clare and whether she is better."

The next evening as Francis rode up to the castle, light was streaming from all the windows, and he could hear laughter and music. At the gate and along the walls, there were flaming torches which made the scene as bright as day. When he entered, Francis saw many people gathered in the great stone hall where a big fire burned at one end. A long table was set with food and drink. The Lady Ortolana and her husband were seated on rich chairs raised above the level of the floor. Francis went forward to greet them. As he bowed low, the Lord Faverone said:

"You are most welcome, Francis—both you and your lute."

Then he called to a young man who was standing nearby:

"Orlando, this is Francis Bernardone. He has come to sing for you on your eighteenth birthday."

Francis looked up to see a tall youth with light hair, a thin face, and a merry smile. At once he knew that they would be friends. The Lady Ortolana was holding a little girl on her knee and smiled at him as he bowed again.

"You can see," she said, "that Clare is already much better from the brew which your kind mother sent us."

"My mother will be pleased," answered Francis, "for she hoped especially to hear this. And now, having seen for myself, I may also tell my mother that the Lady Clare truly looks like a little golden angel. In heaven itself there can be none more beautiful!"

Again he bowed, and the little girl stretched out her small hands to him as though she had understood. Then the Lord Faverone said with a laugh to Orlando:

"Here, nephew, if this young man can make such pretty speeches to the ladies, he should be introduced to all of them!"

So Orlando led Francis around the hall to the maidens who stood about, laughing and chatting with their friends. Then he took him over to a corner where several young men were standing.

"These are my special friends," he said, "Matteo, Armando, Antonio, and Giorgio. This is Francis."

Never had he met so merry a group. Although they were older than he, they made him feel welcome. Soon he was joining in their laughter and was pleased to find himself as quick at jokes as were they. As the servants passed in and out, serving the wine, the Lord Faverone came over and asked Francis if he would sing. So Francis took his lute and stood by the fireplace and began to sing a tale about King Arthur and his knights.

At first, only a few seemed to hear him, and it was hard to sing against the noise and the laughter. But soon, as the clear young voice rose louder, all became silent and leaned forward to listen. When he had finished, there was a great clapping of hands. Orlando and his friends surrounded him, all trying to tell him at once how much they had liked it. And Orlando exclaimed:

"After this, Francis must come to all our feasts!"

Francis felt very happy indeed that he had pleased the young nobles and had made such fine new friends. The feasting and the dancing went on gaily until very late, and at last he thought it was time that he should go home. But as he made his way to say good night to his hosts and to thank them, Orlando stopped him.

"My friends and I are going for a ride by moonlight and want you to join us."

Francis was delighted, as he really did not like to have such a happy evening come to an end. So off went Orlando to find Matteo, Armando, Antonio, and Giorgio. Soon, in the crisp night air and under the bright moon, the six youths were racing their horses at a mad

pace through the fields. Raphael in his own way let
Francis know that he was enjoying it as much as his
master. He tossed his head as though saying: "It's good
to be young, and in Assisi, isn't it?" Finally, breathless,
they drew up under a big tree. Matteo wiped his brow
and said, laughing:

"There is nothing like a moonlight gallop to clear a
man's head of wine."

"But," said Armando, "we can't go home yet. It is
Orlando's eighteenth birthday, and we've only half celebrated it. Let us ride into town. Surely we can find some
fun there!"

Every one agreed, so the six horses galloped on—
through the market square and into the heart of the
sleeping city. Not a soul was in sight. Every one had
been in bed for hours, and, except for the sound of their
horses, everything was very still. Orlando held up
his hand for them to stop just near the cathedral of
San Rufino.

"I have it in mind," said he, "that it would be fun
to awaken the *podesta* whose house lies just over there.
That fat old man has been getting too much sleep of
late and it's not good for him."

They all thought this was a fine idea, but just how
should it be carried out? Suddenly Francis looked up
at the great bell of the cathedral, which hung high
above their heads.

"There is nothing," he said, "that would awaken the
podesta as nicely as the ringing of that bell."

3

"Francis," said Orlando, "you are very wise for your years. The bell is the very idea!"

"We have but to enter the church and pull the long rope that hangs in the little room at the back," said Francis. "Let us go and explore. Now every one be quiet and stop laughing."

Softly they dismounted and tied their horses to the posts in front of the cathedral. But when they had tiptoed up to the great doors, they found them locked. Now they all looked to Francis, feeling sure that he would know what to do.

"Wait here," he whispered, "while I run around to the back. Perhaps they have forgotten to lock the little door there. If I don't return in a moment, you will know that I'm inside. When you hear the bell, jump on your horses quickly and be off before the *podesta* sees you."

"But what about you?" asked Orlando.

"Raphael has wings. I'll get away in time. Don't worry."

They stood there, waiting in the dark and in the stillness and trying not to laugh out loud. Orlando whispered, "That Bernardone! He's ready for anything!"

Just then there broke upon the quiet night such a wild clamoring from the big bronze bell above their heads as to awaken the dead. Orlando, Matteo, Armando, Antonio, and Giorgio flew to their horses while the long peals shattered the silence. Windows began to open, heads to pop out as they dashed away.

Inside the church, Francis clung on to the bell rope. He might as well make a good noise while he was about it. But he hung on to the rope longer than was wise. Finally, he let go, and, in his hurry to get out, he stumbled in the dark against a bench. By the time he had picked himself up and was running to get Raphael, there were lights in the *podesta's* house. As he swung himself into the saddle, two men ran out from the stable with flaming torches held high above their heads. Then the door of the house opened, and out ran the fat *podesta* himself, clad only in his nightshirt and nightcap. Before Francis could get away, the torches were casting a glow of light all about him. At once the *podesta* recognized that fine black horse and knew whose it was.

"Young Bernardone!" he cried in a loud voice as he shook his fist after Raphael's vanishing tail. "I'll see your father about this! And you yourself shall answer to me in court!"

The last thing Francis heard was the shouts of laughter from the heads which had appeared at all the windows. In the light of the torches, the angry *podesta* with his red beard, standing in the middle of the road in only his nightshirt and nightcap, and shaking his fist, was a sight to make anyone laugh.

But Francis was not laughing as he took the dark road down the hill. What had he done now? He dropped his head, and, in the moonlight, the ruby in the dragon's mouth glowed up at him. Perhaps his mother had been right. Perhaps dragons *were* bad luck. His father would

be furious; and Francis was very frightened of his
father when he was angry. The *podesta* would make a
terrible fuss. Suddenly, for no reason, the thought of
Leo, his new friend from the farm, popped into his
head. Somehow he knew that Leo would never have
done such a thing; and all at once he felt terribly
ashamed. He hoped that Leo would never learn of it.
But no, the whole town, including the school, would,
in a few hours, be buzzing with the story. And how
his gentle mother would grieve! His father would surely
beat him and might even lock him up in the little
dungeon. . . .

Perhaps he had better not go home at all. Perhaps he
and Raphael had better spend the rest of the night down
on the plain, and, as soon as it was light, make their way
northward, on and on, until they could reach the faraway Alps and could cross them into safety. He turned
Raphael down the steep hill that led to the plain.

THREE

The Tavern of The Three Angels

FOUR years later, in the year 1201, a snowy Christmas Eve had come to rest upon Assisi. Just outside the city gates there lay a tavern called "The Three Angels"; but those who went there were anything but angels. Filippo, the manager, had once been a member of a band of brigands who hid on the mountainside, lying in wait to rob innocent travelers.

It worried the *podesta* that Filippo had chosen to set up a tavern so close to the city gates. But since Filippo had promised never again to be a brigand, and since what went on *outside* the gates was really none of the *podesta's* business, Filippo had been allowed to remain. Nevertheless, the *podesta* would have given anything to be rid of him, for The Three Angels had soon become the meeting place of all the wild youths of Assisi.

On this Christmas Eve, two travelers, their horses wet with snow, rode up the dark hill from the plain on their way to the city. Rounding a curve, they saw the tavern's lights casting their glow across the road and heard the sound of laughter coming from within. One said to the other:

"Shall we go in to warm ourselves and have something to eat before we push on to Assisi?"

"We might as well," answered the other. "It has been a long, cold ride from Perugia and it is late. By the time we reach the monastery, the monks will all be abed and we cannot hope for any food there until morning."

In those days, there were not many inns along the road where strangers might pass the night with safety. Most people preferred to stay at the monasteries where the monks always had a place and a welcome for travelers.

"This tavern has an evil reputation," murmured one as they crossed the courtyard, "so keep a hand on your dagger."

When they opened the door, a gale of laughter and singing floated out into the cold night. Filippo himself came forward to greet them. He led them to a small table close by the roaring fire. Once, long ago, Filippo had lost an eye in a fight with another brigand and, ever since, he had worn a large, black patch to cover the place. It gave him a rather terrifying appearance.

Just off the main room of The Three Angels there was another, smaller room, and it was from there that the noise was now coming. The door stood open, and the travelers looked curiously toward it. Inside, they could see a long table about which were gathered a dozen young men. At its head sat a handsome youth with laughing brown eyes, who wore a crown of gilded leaves pushed far back upon his head. There was something about him that made the travelers stare.

"That one," said Filippo as he poured out their wine, "is young Francis Bernardone, the son of the merchant. He is my best customer," he added proudly, "and already, at nineteen, he spends money like a prince. Lucky for him that his father is rich! He brings his friends here almost every night. And tonight they have crowned him King of the Revels!"

At that moment Francis pushed the gilded leaves still farther back upon his head and made a remark which sent all the young men into gales of laughter. Now they were calling for more wine, and Filippo hurried away to get it.

"If what we see," said one of the strangers to the other, "is a fair sample of the noble youths of Assisi. . . ." He broke off and leaned forward to whisper to his companion: "When the hour strikes, our Perugian knights will make short work of them!"

"Hush!" said the other, laying his hand on his dagger and looking around fearfully.

In the other room Orlando had now risen to propose a toast:

"To Francis!" he cried, holding his glass high, "to our King of the Revels! Long may he reign!"

Then Matteo, Armando, Antonio, and Giorgio all jumped to their feet to repeat Orlando's words, and all drank to Francis. One of the group called out:

"A song, oh King!"

So Francis took his lute and, leaping upon the table, began to sing a jolly tune in which they all joined. When he had finished, he cried:

"It is Christmas Eve, a night for revels! What is your pleasure, my subjects? How shall we make merry, and where shall your king lead you?" Then he pointed to a heap of clothing which had been thrown upon a bench. "We have here," he said, "the costumes of *jongleurs* which I brought along in case. . . ."

He was interrupted by cries of, "To town, to town! And dressed as *jongleurs!*"

Now there was a wild scramble for the costumes and much merriment as they strove and snatched among themselves for the best. They pulled the strange garments over their rich doublets and set the gay hats with bells upon their heads. Each covered his face with a comic mask. That of Francis showed the head of a grinning bear. At the noise, Filippo rushed in and bent double with laughter as he saw the young nobles strutting about in their odd clothes. Francis threw a purse of gold upon the table and then they all sped off through the tavern door, leaving it open behind them. A cold blast fell upon the two travelers from Perugia. As one of them went to close the door, he could hear the young men's horses pounding toward the city gates.

"It will be anything but a quiet Christmas Eve in Assisi," he remarked softly to his companion.

Now at that moment, nearly every one in the city was on the way to attend Midnight Mass at the cathedral of San Rufino. The riders from the tavern tied their horses near the church. Francis posted his men in the shadows where they could step out suddenly and startle the good townspeople on their way to Mass. They were to dance and to jest. They were to snatch the caps from the men's heads and even kisses from the maidens. Soon the fun began. Francis was everywhere at once, making jokes and fun. In spite of his mask, many people recognized him.

"That's young Bernardone," they said, laughing. "You can always tell *him* by his pranks!"

Now, high above, the great bronze bell of San Rufino began to ring—the same bell which, only four years ago, had caused him so much trouble. But he did not want to think about that now. And then, just as the last peal rang out, too late he remembered that he had promised to meet Leo at Midnight Mass. Well, it couldn't be helped now. How could he have known that his friends were to carry him off to The Three Angels? It was too bad, but just as soon as he could, he would ride over to the farm and make things right with Leo.

In the four years that had passed since he had first met this friend, Leo had finished school and was now staying on the farm helping his father. Francis had missed him, for, when Leo had come to Assisi every day, Francis had often met him after school. And whenever he had ridden to Spoleto on errands for his father, he had always stopped off for an hour or two at the farm. Sometimes Leo's father would let his son take the old farm horse, Beppo, and the two youths would ride over to Spoleto together. At such times, Raphael was always very polite to Beppo and kept at a slow pace so as not to make it hard for him to keep up.

The holidays in Assisi were so gay that it was a full two weeks after New Year's Day when Francis rode through the city gates to see his friend. The ground was still muddy from the snow, and Raphael picked his way daintily around the puddles. Francis was glad that he did, for he was wearing a new velvet cloak of blue, and he did not want it spattered with mud. After the fashion of the day, he had combed his long hair carefully and had sprinkled it with rose-water, as all the young nobles did.

He was feeling very pleased with himself until,

suddenly, just beyond the gates, he saw something which made him go cold with fear. There, just ahead of him, three creatures were gathered at the side of the road —a man, a woman, and a child. Their heads, arms, and legs were covered with bandages, and the man and the little boy stood on crutches. When they saw Francis, they called out and came toward him with their hands outstretched for money. But Francis pulled Raphael to a short stop.

He knew at once who they were, for the odor which came from their poor bodies was already choking him. They were lepers, ill with the dread disease which had made them outcasts. They were doomed to live forever outside the city and to beg their bread as best they could. People ran when they saw them, for fear that they, too, would catch the terrible disease. There was no cure for it.

Francis quickly turned his horse from the road and set off at a gallop through the fields. But their pitiful cries pursued him, so he stopped and rode back slowly. Keeping as far away as he could, he threw some coins at their feet and then turned again quickly and rode off as fast as Raphael could carry him. His heart was beating with fear and he felt quite sick from the sight of the poor dirty lepers. He, Francis Bernardone, might become a leper himself if he went too close to such as these! It would be much better to die than to live as a leper. Of what use then, would be all his rich clothing and the golden ring upon his finger? He glanced down at it proudly, and the ruby in the dragon's mouth glowed back at him.

While Francis was thinking of these things as he rode along, back in the city his mother and Maria were returning from the market. As they passed the church of San Giorgio, they met one of his mother's friends and the Lady Pica stopped to speak with her. It was the wife of the *podesta*.

"My poor friend," said she to the Lady Pica, "my husband and I feel very sorry for you. This son of yours, Francis, must be a constant worry!"

"Not at all," replied the Lady Pica, drawing herself up and holding her chin high. "Why should you say that?"

"Why, although he is almost a man now, he still thinks of nothing but gay times and wild doings. Between him and his noble friends, the town is in a constant uproar. What sort of man will he become?"

"You will see," answered the Lady Pica firmly, "that he will yet become a very great Christian!"

The *podesta's* wife shook with laughter.

"My dear friend, you are indeed a loving mother. But who knows? You may be right. While my husband is always angry at Francis for disturbing the peace, I would not for anything have missed seeing his antics on Christmas Eve. He and his friends had the whole town laughing. And your son has more spirit than any of them!"

At that moment, Raphael, with Francis on his back,

was trotting across the plain toward the farm. They were drawing near a clump of trees and Francis said to his horse:

"Look well at those trees, Raphael, and you will remember them. We tried to sleep under them that night four years ago when we rang the cathedral bell and awakened the *podesta*. We were running away. Don't you remember how cold it was?"

Raphael flicked his ears.

"And how, as the hours passed, we began to think that it would be a long journey over the Alps to freedom? And that it would be much warmer at home?"

Raphael began to trot faster.

"So, when it was light, we decided to go home after all and to face the *podesta* and my father's beating. We never felt more miserable in our lives. We knew we had been bad boys. Lucky for you that my father did not beat you, too!"

Raphael tossed his mane and snorted.

"You needn't snort like that. You were in it just as much as I. And you laughed as hard as anyone at the way the *podesta* looked!"

Raphael gave a loud whinny. Francis was smiling at the memory. As usual, his mother had taken his part and had saved him from being cast into the little dungeon. She had even gone to the *podesta* and made him promise not to hold a public trial.

Now, as they drew nearer to the farm, Francis began to feel very sorry for the way he had treated Leo on

Christmas Eve. What could he say to make it right with him? He had gone off with his noble friends and had left Leo alone and waiting. Whence came this spirit of mirth which always swept over him at the wrong times? It made him forget everything but fun. But afterwards, when it was too late, he was always sorry. Would Leo forgive him? Francis was afraid, thinking of all the angry things his friend could say. He almost turned Raphael around and started for home again. But the trees back there on the plain had reminded him that running away from things did not help. You only had to face them later. So, even though he was afraid, he rode on. He told himself that he would soon be a knight and so must show the courage of a knight.

When they reached the farm, there was no one in sight but Beppo, the old horse, who was munching hay in an open shed. Francis dismounted, and Raphael strolled over to rub noses with Beppo. Just then Leo came running across the field, and Francis began to be frightened all over again. How could he ever explain? But then he saw that Leo was wearing his sunniest smile.

"Francis!" he called joyously. "I'm so glad you've come!"

At once Francis knew that Leo had forgiven him. When he started to make excuses, Leo only interrupted, laughing:

"Come, come; no explanations are needed between friends! I knew that you had to be with the young nobles, for are you not soon to become a knight?"

So Francis felt happy again, and the two sat down on a big rock. Francis began to tell Leo of all the pranks they had played on Christmas Eve. Leo laughed heartily. How good it was to have a friend like Leo, thought Francis. He always understood everything.

Then Leo said:

"How would you like it if I rode back to Assisi with you? I have some grain to deliver to the Benedictine monastery on the mountain."

"Splendid!" cried Francis. "I can see that Beppo is longing to go on a journey with Raphael. And when we have finished your errand, you must stop and have supper with us. My mother and father would be greatly pleased."

So Leo went to the shed to pick up a sack of grain which he tied to Beppo's saddle. Then he set out for Assisi with Francis. They went along at a slow pace, for Beppo had more of a load than usual. But this gave the two friends a chance to talk.

"This is like the time you carried me home from school," said Leo, "for Raphael went just as slowly as this until you set him to dancing with that ridiculous French song!"

"That was to punish you for not telling what you wanted to do when you grew up," replied Francis. "By the way, you never *have* told me!"

Just then, mounting the hill, they came in sight of the city gates.

"I hope the lepers have gone away," said Francis,

making the sign of the cross. "They gave me a real fright."

"Poor souls," sighed Leo. "If only our Lord would cure them as He did when He was upon earth!"

It was a great relief to Francis when he saw that the lepers had disappeared. As they passed the tavern of The Three Angels, Filippo, with his black patch, stuck his head out of the window.

"A fair day to you, Master Francis!" he cried, grinning from ear to ear. "And will you be dining here tonight? We have such a pie! All made of young larks. It is so good that even the larks in it are singing!"

"Not tonight," called Francis, laughing, "but soon. That Filippo," he murmured to Leo, "he takes every penny my father gives me—like the true bandit he is. Yet I cannot help but like him. He always makes me laugh."

They had almost reached the gates when a small, shabby church came into view.

"Let us stop here," said Leo, "and go into the church of San Damiano to pray for a while.

Francis looked at his friend in surprise.

"In that little, broken-down church?" he asked. "Why look, it's all falling to pieces! Most of the windows are out, and it must be filthy inside!"

"But it's a real church," protested Leo, "and our Lord is present there, even if the priest is too poor to keep it in repair."

Francis laughed at him.

"I've no mind to soil my new velvet cloak, church or no church," he said. "I'll tell you what. If you wish to pray, we can visit the monastery church after you have delivered the grain. It has many beautiful things, and the monks make the lay brothers keep it very clean."

Leo agreed and they rode along through the town, turning up the steep road that led to the monastery almost at the top of Mount Subasio. They climbed and climbed and, finally, came to the large clearing where stood the monastery buildings, surrounded by rich farmlands. The buildings and the fine church were of massive stone. Here and there monks, in black robes and with cowls over their heads, were walking about, reading their prayer books.

After Leo had delivered the grain, the two youths entered the church. Francis walked about, examining the paintings and the fine images, but Leo dropped to his knees and bent his head in prayer. When they came out, the sun was just going down in a golden haze, and the huge monastery bell was tolling the Angelus. The monks stopped walking to pray and Francis and Leo stood in the shadow of the porch. As the bell stopped tolling, a great company rode into the courtyard. It was the abbot himself, the head of the monastery, riding a splendid horse which was covered with a blanket of crimson velvet. About the abbot's neck hung a heavy gold chain set with jewels. After him rode several monks. The abbot was returning from a visit to another monastery.

When he saw the young men standing there, he drew up his horse, smiled, and held out his hand. Francis and Leo ran forward to kiss the great golden ring upon his finger. Then the abbot gave them his blessing and the two youths, thanking him, went off to find their horses.

On their way down the mountainside, Leo turned to Francis and said:

"Now I can tell you what I could not tell you that day, four years ago, when we first met. My dream, which at that time seemed so impossible, has come true. I am going to become a priest."

Francis was so startled that he almost fell off Raphael's back.

"A priest!" he exclaimed. "Why, Leo—no, not you! You can't do that!"

"Why not?" asked Leo, smiling.

"Because—because it would change everything. We would not be able to do things together. I would never see you!"

"Nonsense," said Leo. "Of course you will see me. That is, when I return from my studies."

"Return from your studies? But where are you going?" demanded Francis, suddenly quite angry at Leo.

"To Bologna," answered Leo. "All these years my good father has worked and saved to let me do this thing. I, too, have worked and saved. And now we have just enough money to let me go to Bologna. Of course I shall have to work there, too, while I'm studying."

Francis felt a great heaviness within him.

"When do you go?" he asked.

"Tomorrow."

The word was a great shock to Francis. They rode along in silence for a time. At last Francis said:

"Well, I hope you can be a monk so I won't have to worry about whether you have enough to eat and a warm bed in which to sleep." Then he brightened. "Perhaps some day you can become an abbot, like the one we just left, and can wear fine jewels and have servants!"

"Oh, no," said Leo. "I want to be a simple priest. I may be just as poor as that poor priest of San Damiano."

"That's very foolish," said Francis crossly. "Why be poor when one can as easily be rich?"

But Leo did not answer, for just then they reached the Bernardone house. All through supper the Lady Pica, who was always glad to see Leo, kept wondering why the two friends were so silent. Leo seemed calm and happy. But her Francis—something was wrong with him. Where were all his jokes and lively talk? Where was that gay smile and ready laughter? Long after Leo had gone home she was still puzzling over it.

"Something is troubling our son," she said to Pietro Bernardone when they were alone.

But Pietro, who was thinking about business, said that he had not noticed anything.

The next morning Francis had no time to think about Leo. As he and Angelo left the house, the great bell of San Rufino began to toll. It was the signal which all

Assisians knew meant that everyone must come at once
to the market place to hear news of great importance.
In much excitement the people began to run, and Francis
and Angelo joined them.

"It must be the Perugians," panted Angelo, finding
it hard to keep up with Francis.

When they reached the square, the *podesta* with his
red beard and gold chain was standing on the steps of
the ancient temple which the Roman conquerors had
built there long ago.

"We must arm!" he was shouting to the people.
"Make ready for battle! The Perugians are coming to
attack our city!"

Francis felt his heart beating wildly. This was the
moment for which he had longed. Now he could show
how bravely he could fight. Now he could prove that
he was worthy to be a knight. Gaily he turned to Angelo
and cried:

"We will fight and win! They shall not enter our
gates! . . . Why, Angelo, what's the matter?" He saw
that his brother's face had turned gray and that he was
trembling.

Just then Francis heard the *podesta* say:

"All the men who can fight will meet here in half
an hour. Come fully armed. The knights, on their horses,
will wait at the right side; the men on foot will form in
the rest of the square and in the streets. Count Roland
of Chiusi will command the knights. Make haste, for
we must meet the enemy down below on the plain.

We must defeat them before they can climb the hill to the city. And all should thank God that our good spies have warned us in time!"

Francis knew that Assisi had kept spies in Perugia to watch for the moment that all had known must come. One of them must have slipped out of the city, while it was still dark, to gallop across the plain with the news. There had been unrest in Assisi. The poor people had resented the nobles, their wealth, and their power. They had even attacked some of the great castles. The Sciffi family had been forced to flee. The Perugians had seized this moment to make war, hoping that many of the common people would fight on their side. Now Francis made a vow in his heart that Perugia would never capture Assisi. He and his horse, Raphael, would see to that!

As he turned to join the shouting, running crowd, some one touched his elbow. Count Roland of Chiusi, the knight who always bought the richest of his father's silks, was at his side.

"Francis," he said, "you will ride with the young nobles. Join us here as quickly as you can."

Francis was overjoyed, for this meant that he would fight at the side of his friends, Orlando, Matteo, Armando, Antonio, and Giorgio. When he turned to tell his brother of his good fortune, he found that Angelo had vanished. He ran home, but even before he went in to speak to his parents, he fed Raphael and brushed him from head to hoof.

"We are going to fight for Assisi, my friend," he sang,

as he combed out Raphael's fine mane, "and you must look your bravest! No, you need not prance about just yet. Wait until we reach the field of battle. Then you are to show those Perugian horses how much better you are than they!" (He had forgotten that Raphael himself had been born in Perugia.)

Inside the house his mother was waiting, and there were tears in her eyes. Maria and Lucia stood by, weeping and wringing their hands. His father himself strapped Francis's sword and dagger at his waist; and his mother slipped on his finger the golden ring with its dragon and ruby, pledge of friendship with the Sciffi.

"The Lady Ortolana always said that you were to wear this in battle; and that if you were fighting for truth and justice, it would keep you safe. Do not lose it, my son!"

"Have no fear, *Mamma Mia*," cried Francis, embracing her gaily. "Alone, Raphael and I will send the Perugians flying!"

With a smile he knelt to receive his father's blessing. Angelo was nowhere to be seen. Then Francis was off, leaping into the saddle and waving his plumed cap to them as Raphael stretched out his long legs into a gallop.

When they reached the market square, Francis found that he was the first to join Count Roland, who sat waiting there upon his great brown horse, with the sunlight dancing upon his shining armor.

Presently they were joined by the handsome knight,

Bernard of Quintavalle, an elderly lawyer of great wealth and dignity, who greeted Francis courteously.

Count Roland, who had fought in many a war, really lived in Chiusi, some miles away, but he loved Assisi and had offered to lead its army. Now he rode back and forth as the lines formed and told his men the plan of battle. Francis, the youngest of all in the company of nobles, listened carefully. Once he turned his head to look down over the parapet. In the distance, far away, he could see a large, dark shadow on the plain. As he gazed, it seemed to be moving toward them. His heart began to beat very fast, for then he knew that the shadow was really the Perugian army, marching to attack his city.

Just then the bishop of Assisi, a gentle old man with white hair, went up the steps of the Roman temple and turned to face the square. It was now packed with horsemen and their shining lances, and was bright with gay banners fluttering in the breeze. A great silence fell upon all as the bishop began to pray aloud. He raised his thin white hand in blessing and all bowed their heads. Then Count Roland issued the command and, two by two, the knights rode out of the square and toward the city gates. The soldiers followed.

As Francis rode past the bishop, he looked at him and felt happy when the bishop gave him a warm smile. Something in that smile made him think of Leo who must now be well on his way to Bologna. For the first time he was glad that Leo had gone. Whatever might happen today on the plain there below, Leo would be safe.

When they drew near the gates, all the people of Assisi were waiting to call out their blessings. He caught a glimpse of his mother and father, with Maria and Lucia and Roberto. As they passed the tavern of The Three Angels, Francis was delighted to see Filippo run out. In each hand he waved a huge knife.

"I'll be fighting with the soldiers, Master Francis," he cried. "Then it will be 'Good-by, Perugia!' " At this, with one of the knives, he thrust out at the air before him. He looked so fierce and so frightening, with his black patch over one eye, that Francis, and Orlando who was riding beside him, laughed heartily.

"Good luck, Filippo!" they called back to him.

When they drew nearer the plain, Francis could see that the black shadow had come much closer to Assisi. It seemed like a very large army, with the knights riding before it and the long lines of soldiers behind. Francis looked back at their own army. It was not nearly as large and, for the first time, he began to feel afraid. But then he thought: "Even if we have not as many men, still, we are much braver than the Perugians and we will win—in any case!" That thought made him feel much better. Raphael seemed to be enjoying it all tremendously. He was full of life and Francis found it hard to hold him in.

"Patience, patience!" Francis said to him. "In just a

short time you'll have plenty of chance to snort and run when you chase the Perugians back to their city!"

"Give us a song, Francis," cried Matteo, who was riding just behind them.

Francis lifted his head and began to sing the gay French tune which had so greatly cheered Leo on that day when he had ridden behind Francis. Soon his friends were joining in the chorus. At the jolly music, Count Roland looked back and smiled. "I only hope they can fight as well as they can sing," he prayed.

They were now riding across the plain and soon the count held up his hand for the army to halt. He rode back to give his last orders and to arrange his men.

"Whatever happens," he cried to the knights, "don't let the enemy take your horses!"

Now the black mass had come so near that they could hear the Perugians shouting and could almost see their faces. Not far from a clump of thick trees, Count Roland again held up his hand.

"We halt here," he said, "to wait for them. Then each man must fight with all his strength for Assisi!"

Ever afterwards Francis wondered how he had lived through the next ten minutes. He sat there on Raphael, his hand on his sword, his heart pounding wildly, and waited for the Perugians to charge. He tried to remember all the things he had been taught about how to use his sword, and how to handle his dagger, and how to turn Raphael quickly. But somehow he couldn't remember a thing. Then came a sound he first thought was thunder, but the next instant knew was the hoofs of the enemy's horses galloping toward them. After that, he remembered only swinging right and left with his sword among the Perugian knights.

He had managed to fight off two of them when he felt a stunning blow on his back and suddenly found himself rolling over in the dust, with Raphael looking down at him in surprise. All about him there were men who had fallen. Cries and groans filled the air. He scrambled to his feet, but before he could mount again, a huge soldier lunged toward him. Francis stepped quickly in front of Raphael and faced the man with his dagger. He was bigger and fiercer than Filippo himself, and Francis was no match for him. Suddenly the soldier dropped his dagger and lunged forward to grasp the slim young body. But Francis stepped quickly aside and the huge man went sprawling to the ground. He lay there on his face, gasping for breath. Francis was about to drive his dagger into his back when three other Perugians closed in upon him. He stood in front of Raphael and tried to fight them off. They, too, were bigger than he, and now he knew that he had only a little time.

As he fought with his dagger in his right hand, he managed with his left to trip up one man with his sword. He dodged a blow from another's dagger and plunged his own into the man's arm. The Perugian drew back with a roar of pain. But now the third man was towering over him. Suddenly he dropped and grasped Francis about the knees, throwing him to the ground. Then he leaped forward and grasped Raphael's reins. Raphael whinnied and pranced and tugged to get free. Breathless, Francis rose to his knees and, summoning all his strength, brought his sword down with full force upon the reins, slashing through them and freeing Raphael. They might take him, but they would never take his horse!

"Run, Raphael, run!" he cried. "Run home—home!"

Raphael leapt with a mighty bound over a Perugian who was struggling to his knees and was off like the wind. There was no other horse on the field of battle which could catch him. And well he knew the way home, thought Francis thankfully, as the three Perugians, robbed of their prize and roaring with anger, closed in upon him.

FOUR

The Prisoner of Perugia

It was very cold in the dungeon in Perugia. Water dripped from the stone walls and the rough floor was always wet. It was dark, too, for there was only one window set very high. One could hardly call it a window; it was really just a slit in the thick wall.

There were six of them there in the dungeon: Orlando, Matteo, Armando, Antonio, Giorgio—and Francis. And all were knights except Francis, the youngest. They had been there ever since the Perugians had won the battle on the plain. That was only a month ago, but it seemed like a year to Francis. He could not even remember how he came to be there. His last memory was of the three Perugians setting upon him with their daggers, the sound of Raphael's flying hoofs, and the certainty that they would kill him.

The next thing he had known was awakening in the dungeon. As bad as was the news that Assisi had been defeated, he had rejoiced to find that he was alive and with his friends. While many had been killed, the Perugians had made captives of the nobles and were holding them as hostages.

On a day in February, the prisoners were again discussing the battle.

"You can thank your lucky stars that Raphael was with you," said Matteo, "for by this, they took you to be a knight and did not kill you."

"I am thanking my lucky stars, and Raphael, too!" exclaimed Francis.

"You were a pretty sight when they brought you in here," said Armando. "Your arm was bleeding and you had fainted. They had slung you across the back of a horse, without so much as binding your wound."

"But the jailer gave us water and bandages. When we threw water in your face, you opened your eyes," added Antonio.

"And thought that I was drowning!" laughed Francis.

Then a shadow passed over his face. He remembered that moment of his awakening. He had looked down and noticed that the golden ring with the dragon was no longer on his finger. The pledge of friendship with the Sciffi family was gone. Now he glanced over at Orlando, sitting apart from all the rest, and with his back against the wall. Orlando was one of the Sciffi, and he had behaved very strangely here in the dungeon.

"You were lucky, too," Matteo said, "that your wound was no worse."

"It is healing nicely," said Francis, looking down at his bandaged arm. "I'm most grateful to all of you and to our good jailer, Giovanni."

Orlando spoke for the first time.

"Good jailer!" he sneered. "You have a strange idea of goodness. What a horrible dungeon these Perugians keep for their prisoners!"

"If you think this is bad," laughed Francis, "you should see our little dungeon at home. It has no window at all, and you can't even stand up in it. I once locked a man in there for saying that the dungeons in France were larger."

"Tell us about it," urged Giorgio.

Francis began to tell them of how he had tricked the French teacher into entering the little dungeon and of how he had laughed over it with the brown hare.

"But," said he, "Master Jacques did not laugh. He swore. Nor did my father laugh when he heard of it. I could not sit down for a week from the beating he gave me!" He made a comical face and rubbed himself tenderly. Everyone laughed but Orlando.

Time dragged heavily in the prison and it was indeed hard to keep up one's spirits. The young men were cold and hungry and homesick. The worst part of all was that the prisoners did not know how long they would have to stay here. Would it be months? Or perhaps even years? Had Assisi forgotten them?

Francis felt all these things deeply, and he knew that the others were suffering as he was. He did his best to cheer them with songs and stories and even dances. And all would laugh and feel better—except Orlando. He only grew crosser and crosser. When Francis would step around the dungeon in a *jongleur* dance, Orlando would say:

"Bernardone, I do believe you've gone mad. I always thought you were lacking in sense. If we ever get out of this place, you will surely be shut up in a madhouse!"

Now it was plain to see that Giovanni, their jailer, had more of a liking for Francis than he had for the others. One day Orlando said to him crossly:

"You old fool! You do anything that Bernardone asks of you. But for the rest of us, nothing! Yet it is *we* who are the nobles of Assisi. He is only the son of a merchant. If you knew what was good for you, you would serve *us* and not the son of a common merchant!"

That night, when the others were all asleep, Francis felt very sad. Though he had not shown it, he had been very much hurt by what Orlando had said. He had always thought that they were good friends. Sadly he rubbed the finger where the ring used to glow.

"I've lost the friendship of the Sciffi," he said to himself. "And my mother was right. The dragon brought only bad luck. Well, I'm glad it's gone if that's the sort of friendship to be expected from the Sciffii."

But the next morning he thought: "I should not be angry at Orlando for what he said yesterday. After all, he said it only because he is unhappy."

From then on, he tried in every way to make Orlando feel better. He sat down beside him and coaxed him to talk about his family and many other things. Gradually Orlando began to smile again.

After many months had passed in this way, one day Giovanni said to Francis:

"A messenger from your father came this morning."

"Oh," cried Francis, "who was it?"

"A man named Roberto. He said he was from your father's shop."

"My good friend Roberto!" cried Francis. "You have not let him go away? I may see him?"

Giovanni shook his head. "It's against orders. But I can tell you all he said."

Francis seized him by the arm. "Tell me, Giovanni! My mother?"

"She is well. They are all well. Even your horse is well and they are giving him good care."

Francis sat down on the floor and began to weep a little from relief. He could not help it.

"Come," said Giovanni briskly, "there is more good news. A truce between Perugia and Assisi has been arranged. We are to have peace for a time. And soon, your father hopes, you will all be released and sent home!"

A wild cheer went up from the prisoners.

"Your leaders, too, are safe: the Count Roland of Chiusi and the knight, Sir Bernard of Quintavalle. Also, your friend, the bandit, Filippo."

Everyone laughed and cheered, and Orlando cried:

"We will celebrate at the tavern on the first night of our return!"

Now that they knew they would be set free, the dungeon seemed quite a different place. All talked constantly of what they would do when they got home. When they asked Francis, he always said the same thing:

"I shall join the Crusades and become a famous knight!"

They spoke, too, about the brides they hoped to win. Francis always said:

"My bride will surpass all others in beauty, virtue, and nobility. . . ."

It was a lovely day in early spring when Francis came home. He had spent more than a year in the dungeon of Perugia, and was very thin. But today the trees were dressed in their best light green, the young flowers were in yellow hats, the birds were singing, and never had the sky above Assisi looked as blue. No one had known just when to expect him, so he opened the front door and ran toward the terrace where, at this hour, he knew he would find his mother and father. As he ran through the kitchen, Maria screamed and dropped a kettle of soup on the floor. Lucia sat down suddenly. Francis waved gaily and kept on running until he reached the terrace.

"I'm home, *Mamma Mia!*" he cried as he hugged her. She wept as she clung to him and whispered:

"Oh, my son, how thin you have grown!"

His father beamed with joy and kept an arm about his shoulder. Such a welcome they all gave him—even Angelo!

"Excuse me a moment," said Francis, "I must say hello to Raphael."

Then he ran out to the stable and flung an arm about Raphael's neck. The horse pranced about, and whinnied, and put his nose on his master's shoulder. He was very glad to see Francis.

Soon friends of the family began to pour into the house, all happy and laughing that Francis was back. Everyone talked at once, and all asked questions at the same moment. Maria and Lucia carried in wine and cakes; and it seemed to Francis that the house had never been so merry. Everyone said that Pietro Bernardone looked ten years younger now that his son was home.

The celebrations in honor of the returned prisoners lasted for two weeks, and Assisi was gay with dancing and singing. Of course there was a feast at The Three Angels, but this time Filippo himself paid for all the wine, grinning from ear to ear as he kept filling the glasses. He made the young men laugh with his boasting of how well he had used the two big knives in the battle. They did not believe all that he told them, but they liked listening to it anyway.

Now Francis went every day to the shop, but his friends kept him out so late at night that often he found he could not get up early in the morning. If he arrived at the shop an hour or two late, Angelo gave him a sour look. But his father only smiled and gave him more money to spend. Everything now seemed as it had in the old days—except that Leo was missing.

One evening soon after his return, Francis was brushing Raphael after making a trip to Spoleto for his father, when suddenly the brush fell from his hand. He was shaking all over and felt very hot.

"I feel so strange, Raphael," he said. "I wonder if I'm going to die."

Raphael turned around and rubbed his nose against his master's arm. With trembling hands Francis gave him his supper. Then, feeling very sick, he found his way to the kitchen and dropped on a bench. Maria gave him one look and then ran for the Lady Pica. They helped him upstairs to bed, and his worried mother sent Angelo hurrying down the street to bring one of the priests of San Giorgio who was very wise about sickness. Then she and Maria quickly brought coverings and a steaming hot mixture which they made Francis drink. He felt very sick indeed. His body seemed to be in the center of a great fire. The kind priest did all he could and then left. The Lady Pica followed him down the stairs.

"Father," she asked, "is he very ill?"

The priest looked at her sadly and nodded his head.

"He is very ill indeed," he said, "and it is no wonder after the long months he spent in that cold dungeon!"

"Father, will—will he die?"

The priest laid his hand on her arm.

"He may. He must have the best of care. And you must be brave—whatever happens."

FIVE

The Last Feast

Now a great stillness settled upon the house of Pietro Bernardone. People walked about on tiptoe and spoke in whispers. The Lady Pica stayed in the sickroom all day and most of the night. Maria and Lucia climbed the stairs with jugs of cool water and mixtures brewed in the kitchen. Pietro Bernardone had lost his smile and could not keep his mind on business. Raphael hung his head and refused to eat.

Francis tossed and burned with fever. He did not know his mother or know where he was. Most of the time he thought he was back in the dungeon of Perugia and cried out strange things which his mother did not understand. One night she was sure that he was dying. She put her ear to his lips and could not hear him breathe. Then she dropped to her knees by his bed and prayed aloud:

"Dear God, I have told others that he would yet live to be a great Christian. Please let him live!"

At last there came a day in June when Francis opened his eyes and knew his mother and smiled at her. He was thinking how pretty she looked, with her blue veil about her head, and her blue eyes now full of joy. The casement was open, and Francis could hear the birds outside talking and singing. And he could even watch them as they fluttered in and out of the plum tree which hung its blossoms near the window. Sometimes he felt that he knew exactly what they were saying.

Mrs. Robin was calling over to Mrs. Thrush:

"You must come and see my new babies—three of them! Two boys and a girl! They just came out of the prettiest blue eggs!"

And Mr. Robin was saying to Mr. Thrush:

"That's my worm! I was here first. Besides, I now have a wife and children to feed! And with the high cost of living . . ."

Francis was still too weak to move so he passed the long hours in bed, thinking about all that had happened to him in his life. He was now twenty-two. No longer a boy, no longer a youth. He would have to make plans for the future, for a man could not go on leading the sort of life he had led up to now. He began to go over it, step by step. All he could remember was pleasure—except for the dungeon of Perugia. Yes, he had done a little work for his father; but that, too, had been fun. His father had been awfully good to him; and of course his mother had always spoiled him. He could not have been much comfort to his father—always in trouble with the *podesta*. And his wild, gay times with the young nobles must have caused his mother much worry. How good she had been to him through his long illness!

Now he wondered whether he, himself, had ever been good to sick people. Suddenly he remembered the lepers. He had always run away from them. That hadn't been very nice. How would he have felt if everyone had run away from him when he was sick? He was dreadfully ashamed when he thought of the lepers. To be sure, he had thrown them money. But what was money? It wasn't his, anyway. It was his father's, earned through hard work. It was one thing to give money to the poor if one had earned it one's self. But to give money earned by *someone else?* Why, anyone could do that.

His father now came in to see him every day and sat by his bed to relate all the latest happenings in Assisi.

"A good result of the truce with Perugia," said Pietro one evening, "is that it has ended the revolt of the people against the nobles. Those who had to flee, have come back now. Your friends, the Lady Ortolana and the

Lord Faverone, with the Lady Clare and the other children, returned some time ago."

"Was the Sciffi palace much damaged?" asked Francis.

"Quite. But it is all repaired now, and soon you will again be there at the feasts you used to enjoy so much!"

To Pietro's surprise, his son was silent.

"Come," said his father, "surely you will be glad to see the Sciffi family again? Orlando has been here several times to ask how you were faring. It's too bad that his cousin, the Lady Clare, is so much younger than you! Already, at the age of ten, she gives promise of being very beautiful. You will soon have to think of choosing a bride, you know!"

Francis smiled at his father.

"What bride would want *me?*" he asked. "I have yet to become a knight and to prove that I am worthy."

"You will. And then you must choose a bride of the highest nobility. She will be glad to have you, for so I have trained you. And never fear, my son, you will be one of the richest young men in Assisi!"

Francis pressed his father's hand.

"You have been very good to me," he said. But there was no smile upon his face.

"Nonsense," said his father. "Cheer up! You are sad and depressed because you have been so ill."

But Francis continued to be sad as he lay there remembering his youth. Even on the day when Maria and Lucia helped him slowly down the stairs and out to the terrace, he could not throw off the sadness. True, he was glad to be out in the sun again and to be gazing up into the trees through their green leaves. He tried to forget his sorrow by listening to the talk of the birds.

When he grew stronger, he was able to go about by himself with the help of a cane. The first thing he did was to make his way to the stable to see Raphael. He stopped in the kitchen first for a honey cake, and when Raphael saw him coming, he pranced and tore at his halter.

"There, there, Raphael," he said, "just eat this honey cake and you will feel better. Soon we will be off together again, far and wide over the hills and the plain. Won't that be fun?"

The next day was as beautiful as are all June days in Assisi. Francis thought he would try taking a little walk. Perhaps if he went to the city gates where he could look out over the plain below and up at the heights of Mount Subasio, he would not feel so sad. His heart was still very heavy, and he wished that Leo would come back from Bologna.

Taking his cane, he started out past the church of San Giorgio and down the hill to the city gates. As he walked along, people greeted him gaily and cried out that they were glad to see him about again. He smiled back at them and thought how kind everyone was. Yet he had never done anything for them. He had made himself only a nuisance in the town.

As he walked along it seemed to him that never before had he passed so many poor people. Some of them were carrying heavy burdens on their backs—sacks of stones which were to be used in rebuilding the damaged palaces. Some of them were pushing great rocks up the hill with their shoulders. All looked tired and thin and ragged. Many were old and sick. He thought of Orlando and his other friends—and of himself. All of them had plenty of money to spend. All lived in fine homes and wore rich clothing. They did no work to earn the good food they ate and the wine they drank; and they wasted their time in pleasure. But then he thought: "When I get to the city gates, and look out again over the beautiful plain and up at the mountain, I will forget this sadness."

He had to go along slowly, but finally he got there. He sat down on a wall to look about at the scene which had never failed to lift his heart. There it was, spread out below him and above him, in all its beauty of green and blossom, and with the soft blue sky hanging over all. For a long time Francis looked at it. But the strange thing was that for once it made him feel no happier. He remembered that only a short distance beyond the gates the lepers hid, praying that some traveler would come along and throw them a few pennies for food. He could not forget the poor workmen pushing the heavy stones, whom he had passed on the road. Well, when he felt stronger, he would ride out on Raphael and see the lepers. And he would try his best not to run away from them—but he was not at all sure that he would succeed.

He slid down off the wall and turned his face toward home. Just then he heard the galloping of horses behind him. As the two riders went by, they suddenly pulled their horses to a stop.

"Francis!" both cried at once.

It was Orlando and Matteo, smiling down at him.

"We're glad you are better and out again!" exclaimed Orlando.

"We thought you would *never* get well!" cried Matteo. "It's the longest eight weeks we have ever spent. The town has not been the same!"

"Nor The Three Angels," laughed Orlando. "Every time we have been there, Filippo has asked about you. The old brigand has been quite sad. It hasn't been any fun at all."

For the first time that day Francis felt happy. He was very glad to see his old friends again. As he smiled up at them, Orlando said: "Come, get up on my horse behind me. We'll take you home. That's a long hill ahead of you."

Francis set a foot in his stirrup, Orlando gave him a hand, and off they started. As they jogged along, Orlando said:

"Matteo will have a birthday next week. What do you say that we celebrate it at The Three Angels?"

"Splendid!" cried Francis. "I myself will give the feast."

But the very next moment he was sorry that he had said it. Somehow he did not think that he would like The Three Angels as much as he had in the past. But Matteo was saying:

"It's very nice of you, Francis! I will tell the others, and we will call for you on Monday evening."

Francis felt glad that Monday was still six days away. Well, anyway, his father would be pleased that he was seeing his old friends again.

The next day Francis felt strong enough to saddle Raphael and go for a little canter. He thought that he would stay away from the streets so as not to see any more poor people. But as luck had it, he soon came upon more of them. They were rebuilding a high stone wall around a handsome palace. Francis knew that it was the home of Sir Bernard of Quintavalle, who had so bravely fought in the battle of the plain. He looked up at the walls of the palace and at the gardens surrounding it. Sir Bernard was very rich. Then he looked at the workmen who were lifting the heavy stones.

They seemed tired and hungry, and he thought that he ought to get off his horse and help them. But, instead, he turned around and rode home. He would take out his lute which he had not touched since he became ill and would sing a little to his mother on the terrace. Perhaps that would make him feel better, and he could forget the poor. . . .

By the time his five friends called for him on Monday evening, he seemed again like the old Francis. He was dressed in a fine new doublet of cloth of gold. His hair was curled and sprinkled with rose-water, and his lute was strung about his neck. He had a purse full of money, and he had made up his mind that he would give his friends a splendid feast. He would sing and make them merry—and he would lose the sadness he was trying to hide.

Filippo always said afterwards that it was the finest feast that Francis had ever given. Orlando had crowned Francis with a wreath of gilded leaves and had put a wand in his hand.

"Behold," he cried to the others, "your King of the Revels!"

Then they all drank to Francis and called for a song. Francis took his lute and, pushing the crown back on his head, began to sing. But instead of the gay song they expected, he sang the beautiful French song of love which the troubadours had taught him. He put such sadness into it that they all felt that something strange had happened to him.

"Come, Francis!" cried Orlando, "you must be in love, for you sound as though your heart were breaking! Give us, now, a merry tune!"

Francis laughed and struck up the jolliest song he knew; and soon they were all singing with him. They raised such a din that Filippo rushed in and begged them to be quiet, as the guests in the other room were complaining.

"Let us go outside," said Francis, "for it is getting very

warm in here and we are bothering others."

"Lead on, Your Majesty," cried Orlando.

Francis, wearing his crown and holding the wand, led his friends outside into the moonlight. There they began to stroll up and down, arm in arm, singing at the top of their voices. But suddenly they missed Francis. They could not see him anywhere.

"Francis, Francis!" they called. "Where are you? Come back, oh King of the Revels!"

Only silence answered them.

"He is playing a joke on us," said Orlando, "and hiding."

So they ran about looking for him, but he was nowhere to be found. At last Armando, who had gone farther than the others, cried:

"Here he is!"

They all came running and laughing, but they stopped short when they saw him. Francis was standing very still, staring into the night as though he were held fast in a dream. He did not seem to see them, for suddenly, before his eyes, there had appeared a face of great beauty. It was a woman's face. It was a face he had never seen before; but all at once he knew that he desired it greatly. It lingered for a moment and then was gone.

As they watched, his friends were frightened. Orlando went up to him and shook him by the arm.

"What is wrong, Francis?" he cried.

"He must be in love!" exclaimed Matteo. "That is the way they all act."

"He's thinking of taking a bride!" cried Antonio.

"Who is she, Francis?" demanded Giorgio.

At last Francis stirred and seemed to hear. He looked around at all of them and smiled.

"You are right," he said. "I am thinking of taking a bride. And she is more beautiful, more pure, more noble, than any of you could ever imagine!"

Suddenly Francis knew that this was the last feast he would ever give at The Three Angels.

SIX

The Search for the Face

THE next morning Francis awakened very early. He had not been able to sleep much for thinking of the face he had seen. Who was she? He did not know her; and yet there was something familiar about her, too. Well, he would search the world over until he had found her.

Rising, he put on his plainest doublet of dark brown. Then he ran softly down the stairs and out to the kitchen where Maria, yawning and sleepy, had just set the kettle over the fire.

"Merciful heaven!" cried Maria. "What are you doing up so early?"

"I have to take a journey. Will you please fix a little breakfast for me?"

As he waited, he spied a cold chicken which had been roasted the day before.

"If you will give me that chicken, Maria," he coaxed, "I will make you a present of my bottle of rose-water."

"That chicken? Why, that's for your lady mother's luncheon! And why do you want a chicken, pray?"

"I am going to see some sick people," replied Francis, "and they are hungry."

"But your mother will be hungry, too," protested Maria. "And what do I want with your rose-water, anyway?"

"You can cook another chicken for my lady mother and have it ready in time. And the rose-water you can give to Lucia."

It seemed like a good bargain to Maria, for Lucia, her daughter, now was being courted by a young man. So she agreed and wrapped up the chicken and put it in a basket. For good measure, she added a loaf of freshly baked bread. Soon Francis and Raphael were on their way to the city gates.

Now as he rode along he prayed that he would find the lepers where he had met them before. He knew they had a house somewhere, hidden from the road; but he did not know where it was. There was still some gold in his purse—left over from the night before. With that, and the basket, the lepers would be pleased. He broke into a merry tune and Raphael began to canter.

When they got beyond the gates Francis could not believe his good fortune. There they were at the side of the road, just as he had seen them before—the woman, the man, and the child. The man and the boy were still on crutches. Before he could help it, Francis had drawn Raphael to a quick stop. As much as he wanted to, could he go on? The same old fear had come upon him. He reached for his handkerchief and held it to his nose. But no; that wasn't very polite. Quickly he put it away again.

Now the lepers had seen him and were hobbling toward him, holding out their hands. With a great effort, Francis rode up to them, smiling. He leaned down and gave them the basket and his purse.

"May God bless you, Master!" they cried joyously.

Then Francis did a surprising thing. He slid off Raphael's back and embraced each one of them. At first they were amazed; and then they wept with joy.

"Master!" they cried, "no one has come near us for years! But this is dangerous for you!"

But Francis only laughed.

"I am your new friend," he said. "And now, please take me to your home."

Very happy that they had found a friend, the three led him to a poor house in the woods where they lived with eight other lepers. Francis sat down and talked with them while they ate the good food.

The gold coins they put in a jar. "This will buy bread for many a day to come," said the man on crutches to the others.

Then they all cried: "God bless you, Master Francis!" —for he had told them his name.

The little boy said shyly:

"That is a very fine horse you have."

"Would you like to ride on him?" asked Francis.

"Oh, yes!" cried the boy, his eyes dancing with delight.

Francis set him up on Raphael's back and led his horse gently up and down. All the lepers watched and laughed and were very happy. When Francis set the boy down again, the child looked up at him and said:

"I think you must be an angel."

"Oh, goodness no!" said Francis, laughing. "But my horse is named for an angel—Raphael, the great Angel of Joy."

The boy reached up and stroked Raphael's nose.

"Good-by, Raphael. Please come back again!" he said.

Francis rode away, promising to return soon. The lepers waved and called to him until he was out of sight. He did not know why it was, but he had never felt so happy. For the first time, the heavy sadness within him had lifted. He set Raphael into a gallop for home. He ran in and bathed himself quickly and changed his doublet.

Pietro Bernardone was greatly pleased to find him

already at work in the shop when he arrived. But Angelo was so surprised that he tripped on the doorstep and almost fell.

"Well, my son, did you have a fine feast last night?" asked his smiling father.

"Oh, yes, my father," said Francis, "and thank you very much!"

Then the door opened to admit two customers. Francis felt that this was surely his lucky day, for they were the Count Roland of Chiusi and Sir Bernard of Quintavalle, both of whom had fought so bravely for Assisi. They greeted Francis warmly, and Count Roland turned to Pietro and said:

"Your son proved to be a very brave soldier. We shall soon make a knight of him."

"Yes," said Sir Bernard. "There is a new Crusade forming, and he can be knighted on the field of battle."

Francis felt his heart dance within him, but suddenly it stopped. All at once he knew that he no longer wanted to become a knight. But his father, smiling and bowing, looked very happy indeed.

"If I could always follow such brave leaders as you, I would be a brave knight," said Francis.

While his father stood chatting with Sir Bernard, he drew out the new silks and spread them before the Count.

When he had made his selections, Count Roland said:

"I hope you will ride over to Chiusi some day and dine with me."

"I should be honored, my lord Count," replied Francis.

Then he turned to Sir Bernard who had now become the first magistrate of Assisi. Francis was happy to show him some black velvet for his robes of office. While they were looking at it, two beggars entered and came up to Francis, holding out their hands. He opened the drawer which held the shop's money and drew out some coins for them.

Sir Bernard smiled, but Angelo, who was standing near by, frowned. After Sir Bernard had left, Angelo turned to his father.

"Francis took money from the till and gave it to those beggars!" he cried angrily.

Pietro Bernardone was very cross.

"You must not do that, Francis," he said. "I give you plenty for your clothing and your friends, but the money is not there for beggars and such!"

Francis knew that it had been wrong to displease his father, but the poor beggars had looked so hungry. Now the sadness fell over him again; and again the beautiful face he had seen the night before came into his mind. If only he knew who she was! If only he could find her, he would be happy again. When Saturday came, he thought he would feel better if he took a long walk in the country.

As he was returning, he again passed the palace of Sir Bernard. There were the workmen still toiling under the hot sun with the heavy stones, rebuilding the wall.

They looked so tired that Francis stopped and said to one who was an old man:

"Will you let me help you?"

The poor man was greatly surprised to see this handsome young gentleman, dressed in fine clothes, offering to help him.

"Why," he answered, looking Francis up and down, "how would a young gentleman like you know how to set stones in a wall?"

"You could show me," answered Francis smiling and taking off his doublet.

The old man began to show Francis how to handle the stones and how to fit them neatly into the wall with mortar. Soon Francis was working almost as quickly as his new friend. After that he came back every afternoon; and the old man was very glad to have his help. One day, as they were working away, Sir Bernard of Quintavalle himself rode out through the gates on his way to hold court. He stopped when he saw Francis setting a heavy stone in place.

"Why, Francis," he exclaimed, "I did not know that you were working on my wall!"

Francis stood up and wiped his brow.

"After the shop, I find it pleasant exercise, Sir Bernard," he said with a smile. "I hope you don't mind."

"Not at all," said Sir Bernard. "But the next time, when I am not off to town, you must come in and have a glass of wine with me."

"I should be honored, Sir Bernard," said Francis.

But even the work on the wall could not banish his sadness; nor bring him nearer to the face he loved.

One Sunday, as he and his mother were leaving church after the early Mass, he felt someone touch his elbow. He turned to see his old friend, Leo, at his side. Right there at the church door, the two friends who had been parted so long hugged each other while the Lady Pica stood by smiling.

"Where—where did you come from?" demanded Francis.

"From Bologna, last night," answered Leo. "I walked here early this morning in the hope of finding you."

"You must join us for breakfast, Leo," said the Lady Pica.

"And you are now a priest?" asked Francis.

"Oh, no, not yet," answered Leo. "And I must return soon to Bologna. I came home only because my father is ill."

"I'm very sorry to hear that," said Francis. "But come along and Maria will give us a good breakfast; and then you shall tell me everything!"

After breakfast, Francis took Leo for a walk. They had so much to tell each other that they were well out in the country before they had finished half. They sat down in a grove of olive trees which hid a large cave in the hillside. Francis told Leo of the face he had seen and of the great sadness he felt.

"Wait for me here a moment," he said, "while I go into that cave to pray."

Francis felt much better when he came out. On their way home, he said:

"It is strange, but the thing that I have wanted all my life—to become a knight—I no longer want. But just the same I would like to go on a Crusade to the Holy Land some day."

"If you give up your plan of becoming a knight, what will your father say?" asked Leo.

Francis sighed. "He will be terribly angry," he said. "I am frightened of what he may do."

Leo stayed on at the farm a few weeks longer until his father was better. Each afternoon he rode over to Assisi on old Beppo. He would leave his horse in the field with Raphael, and the two friends would walk out to the olive grove. There he waited outside the cave while Francis went in to pray. At last the time came when Leo had to go back to Bologna.

"Do not feel sad, my friend," he said to Francis, "for when I finish my studies, I will return; and until then, we will pray for each other."

"You will be so wise by that time," laughed Francis, "and will write and read so well that, should I become a man of business, you can write all my letters for me!"

"Is that so?" asked Leo. "You forget that I'm going to be a priest. You will have to come to me in confession; and then what a fine chance I will have to give you a heavy penance!"

Francis made a face at him and the two said good-by, laughing. It had helped Francis greatly to have Leo with

him, but now he was alone again. He had no wish to
see his gay friends and they did not know what had
come over him. They had grown tired of asking him
again and again to join them at The Three Angels, for
he always said:

"Not tonight. I have some work to do."

"Work!" Orlando would exclaim when he and the
others had gone on without Francis. "That's ridiculous!
What he is really doing is courting. That bride he said
he would take—I wonder who she is? I would give anything to know!"

One afternoon, as Francis was returning from a trip
to Spoleto, he chanced to take the road which led past
the little old church of San Damiano. As he drew near
and saw it still standing there, alone and neglected, he
remembered the day long ago when he and Leo had been
riding along the same road together. Leo had wanted
to stop there and pray, but he, Francis, would not enter
the church lest he soil his fine clothes. Now Francis
pulled Raphael to a halt.

"I am ashamed, Raphael," he said. "I could at least
have gone in and left a few coins for the poor priest.
The church looks even worse now than it did then.
Look at the stones falling out of that wall!"

Now he got off his horse and tied him loosely to an
olive tree. Then he entered the little church of San
Damiano.

At first there was only darkness all about him, and he
stood there, wondering where the altar was. There were

no candles to light the gloom. Even the lamp before the tabernacle, where the sweet Christ lived, was not lit. The priest must be very poor indeed, thought Francis. But gradually his eyes, blinded by the sunshine outside, became used to the darkness. Then he saw the altar at the far end of the church. He looked around. There was no one there but himself.

He walked to the altar and saw that it was very clean and that there were fresh flowers from the fields placed near the tabernacle. Suddenly he felt a love for the priest. Too poor to buy oil for the lamp, he had yet tried to honor the dwelling of his Lord.

Francis dropped to his knees and began to pray. Then he looked up and saw, above the altar, a painted Crucifix. On it there hung the suffering Christ, His arms nailed to the cross. Francis looked up at Christ and began to tell Him of the sorrow which had been his, and of his unhappy search for the face. The silence was deep around him. No one was there but the Saviour of the world and himself.

As he prayed, looking up into the face of his Saviour, suddenly the figure on the cross moved. The beautiful head bent forward, and the eyes looked down into his. In their depths he could see great love. Then the lips moved. And Francis heard clearly the words which came from those lips:

"Go, Francis, and repair My church, which you see is falling into ruin."

SEVEN

The Fairest Lady of Them All

FRANCIS found Father Julio in the garden behind his poor little house next to the church. The old priest was bending over his vines, trying to find a few beans for his supper.

"Father," said Francis, "our Lord has just told me that He wishes me to repair His church."

Father Julio turned in surprise to look at his visitor.

"Why," he said, "are you not young Bernardone, the son of the merchant?"

"The very same, Father," answered Francis, bowing, "and just now, in the church, our Lord spoke to me!" His face was shining with a happiness it had never worn before. There was no longer any sadness in his heart.

The old priest looked at him closely. He knew all about this wild youth, for many had carried tales to him of the gay feasts at The Three Angels and of the pranks played on the *podesta*.

"Come and sit down, my son," he said kindly, as he led Francis to a bench, "and tell me all about it."

Francis related how unhappy he had been and of how he had prayed; and of how, just a short time ago, the Figure on the crucifix had spoken to him.

"And now I am most eager to set about the task my Lord has given me!" he explained.

Father Julio shook his head and murmured:

"It is most strange—strange that our Lord should speak—"

"To me? I know, Father, for indeed I have been a great sinner. But is it not true that He listens even to sinners?"

"Most true, my son."

"So Father, how soon may we begin?"

"But can you do this? You are not a workman. You would have to employ others. It would cost a great deal of money. Besides, your father needs you in his shop."

"My Lord has told me that He needs me here."

The old priest was puzzled. He longed with all his heart to have the church repaired; for many a year he had sorrowed over its decay. But would it not cause trouble between the merchant and his son? Yet Francis was so eager that at last Father Julio was persuaded.

"But how are you to get the money, Francis? You can't ask your father for it."

"No," said Francis, remembering the beggars, "that's true. But I have a few things which I can sell; and then we can start at once! We will need oil for the lamp and candles, and a great many stones and some mortar for the walls."

"It will be very costly," sighed Father Julio who, for years, had been counting over just such expenses.

"Not too bad," said Francis, talking like a man of business. "Don't forget that I will first clean the church. Then I shall lay all the stones myself," he added proudly, "for that is a matter I know something about."

In his heart he was thanking the old workman who had taught him how to repair Sir Bernard's wall. The good priest, feeling happier than he had been in years, bade him good-night and went into his little house, praising God for His goodness in sending the wildest young man in town to help him.

All that night Francis lay awake, planning how he would get the money. He had his lute. He could sell that. He had many fine garments; but perhaps if he sold those, his father would be angry. What else did he own? There was Raphael, of course; but he could not sell *him*. Then he remembered something that Roberto had said to him yesterday in the shop. There was a roll of fine blue velvet, and one of silver brocade, which had just arrived from Paris. He and Roberto had been alone in the shop, and Roberto had put the two rolls away on a shelf, saying:

"Your father intends these for you. They are to be used for some new doublets when you marry your noble lady."

Francis had laughed at Roberto; but now he thought that since the rolls were intended for him, he could sell them, too.

At last he fell asleep, feeling sure that he would have enough to pay for the repair of the church. He would ride over to the market in Foligno early the next morning.

But it proved to be a poor market day in Foligno. Although he had taken the rolls of velvet and brocade with him, as well as his lute, and had sold them all by the end of the afternoon, they had brought a low price. He still needed more money. For the first time since his Lord had spoken to him, he began to feel sad again. He would have to return to Assisi without enough money to repair the church.

Just as he was mounting Raphael, he heard a clatter of hoofs behind him and looked up to see three horsemen enter the market place. It was plain that it was a great nobleman with his servants. Then he heard someone call and saw Count Roland of Chiusi riding toward him.

"Francis," he cried, "what are you doing in Foligno?"

"I came to make a sale, my lord Count," said Francis with a bow.

"Well, if you are ready to leave, why don't you ride back with me to Chiusi? You promised to dine with me, you know; and this is a good chance!"

Francis hesitated. He liked Count Roland very much; but his mind was full of the work he must do on the church. Then he remembered that he still did not have all the money he would need. Perhaps Count Roland could advise him, so he looked up, smiling, and said:

"I shall be happy to come."

"Good! And as it is growing late, you must stay the night at the castle." He turned to one of his servants. "Ride over to Assisi and tell the good merchant, Pietro Bernardone, that his son is spending the night with me in Chiusi."

Francis felt better as he rode along beside Count Roland. He knew that his father would be pleased with the message; and he hoped that Count Roland would help him with his advice. They rode along through lovely country, talking of many things. Count Roland, who liked horses, looked Raphael up and down.

"That's a very fine horse, Francis," he said. "Where did you get him?"

"My father gave him to me when I was fifteen," said Francis. "I think that he bought him in Perugia."

"Well, he's pure Arabian, I should say," remarked the Count. "Let my horse race him in a canter. There's a fine stretch of road before us."

Francis set Raphael into a canter; and Raphael, delighted with the idea, stretched out his long legs and seemed to take wings. They left Count Roland and his fine horse far behind them.

"There, there, Raphael; the race is over now," said Francis, drawing him to a halt. "And you did very well!"

They waited until the Count and his servant rode up.

"Your horse actually flies!" exclaimed the Count.

"Well, he should," said Francis, smiling, "for he bears the name of an angel."

They were riding into the mountains now, and Count Roland pointed ahead to Chiusi, high up on a crest, and to his castle towering above it. Just beyond, there came into view a lofty mountain which soared into the sky like a cathedral candle. It looked mysterious and holy, with the mists clinging all about it.

"What a beautiful mountain!" exclaimed Francis.

"That is the Mount of La Verna," explained Count Roland. "It is a part of my estate, but we use it only for hunting."

Francis looked at it for a long time.

"It must be beautiful up there," he said. "I should love to climb it some day!"

That night, when dinner in the great hall was over, Francis told the Count about his problem and the strange thing that had happened in the church of San Damiano. The Count listened quietly. Francis felt that he could tell him things that he could not tell his own father.

"And so," said Francis finally, "I need more money and I don't know how I can earn it."

"You have nothing more to sell?" asked Count Roland.

"Nothing but my horse," said Francis reluctantly.

"I should not think you would need Raphael while you are rebuilding the church."

"No," said Francis, "and we shall be so poor that I don't even know how I can feed him! You see, my father will be angry with me for leaving the shop, so I cannot live at home. The priest has said that I can share his house until the work is finished."

"Well, Francis," said the Count, "I will buy Raphael from you. He is a fine horse and I will take good care of him. Later, when your work is finished, you may buy him back from me if you like."

Sorry as he was to part with Raphael, Francis was grateful to Count Roland. He knew that here Raphael would have a better home than he could now give him; and he did not feel that he was parting with him forever. The next morning Francis rode Raphael as far as Foligno, for the Count had business there. He said good-by to his friend and to his horse in the market place. One of the Count's men was to ride Raphael back to the castle.

"I cannot thank you enough, my lord Count!" Then Francis put his arm about Raphael's neck and said: "Good-by, Raphael. Be a good horse and do all that the Count asks. And don't feel badly. Be happy because you are helping me to do the task which our Lord has asked of me." Raphael seemed to understand.

Francis, with his purse now full of the money he needed to rebuild San Damiano, set out to walk the long miles to Assisi.

When he reached the church, he went at once to kneel before the crucifix and to tell his Lord that he was very happy that he could now begin the work. As he knelt there, it seemed to him that his Lord was pleased, too, for a great joy flooded his heart. At last he arose and went to the back of the church to look at the broken windows which had been stuffed with rags to keep out the rain and the cold. Just then Father Julio entered and Francis greeted him joyously.

"Look, Father, at all the money we have to repair the church!" he cried as he emptied his purse onto the broad window ledge. "To get it, I sold two rolls of velvet and brocade, my lute, and my horse!"

Father Julio was happy, but he put his hand on the young man's shoulder and said:

"My son, we cannot use this money. Your father would be very angry even though you *did* own the things you sold, for he gave them to you."

Francis felt terribly after all his trouble. But Father Julio said:

"Do not be sad. Leave the money there, and if your father should come, let him take it. It will make things easier for you. And now, let us start to work. If our Lord really wants you to do this task, He will help us."

Francis and the old priest set to work; but as Francis was young and strong, he could do five times as much as Father Julio could. So Francis made him sit down and watch.

First he gave the church a good cleaning. Then Francis went about looking at the holes in the walls and counting the number of stones he would need to fill them. Father Julio went out to the field to find some fresh flowers for the altar. While he was gone, Francis said to the Figure on the crucifix:

"If only we had money to buy oil for the lamp which should always burn before You!"

Suddenly he remembered something. There had been a few coins in his purse before he had sold his possessions. He went over to the window ledge and counted them out. Then he walked into town to see the oil merchant, praying all the time that he would not meet any of his family.

"The oil is for the poor church of San Damiano," he said to the merchant.

The man, a good Christian, made him a very low price for a large jug of oil. Francis had enough money left to buy a few candles and some mortar for the stones. The stones themselves he would pick up in the field behind the church. Luck was with him, for he did not meet anyone he knew.

His joy was very great when he filled the lamp with oil and lit it before the altar. It cast a glow upon the crucifix, and again the suffering Christ seemed to look down upon him with love.

That night when he threw himself on the floor of the priest's house to sleep, he was tired, but very happy. The face of the lady he so greatly loved came before his eyes again and again. If only he knew who she was! Well, perhaps if he prayed long enough, his Lord would reveal the secret.

During the next few days he worked hard, digging up the stones and fitting them into the broken walls. He and Father Julio had very little to eat, but Francis was so happy that he did not care. He was frightened of only one thing—his father's anger.

"He will kill me when he finds out," he said to Father Julio.

"If he should come here, very angry," replied the priest, "I will show you where to hide."

He took Francis down into a secret cellar beneath the church. The door which led to it was hidden by a large painting on the wall. . . .

All this time at home his parents at first had not worried too much about him. They thought that he had stayed on a few days at the castle of Count Roland. But finally they began to wonder why he had not returned.

Then one day the wife of the *podesta* happened to be walking along the country road which passed the church of San Damiano. There she was surprised to see Francis, no longer clad in a fine doublet, but in only his long shirt, and toiling like a workman at the old walls. This was news indeed! Here was the young man whom every one had said would waste his life away in folly. Perhaps his mother's words were coming true that he would yet be a good Christian! On her way home she passed the shop of Pietro Bernardone. Sticking her head in the door, she called out to him:

"I have just seen Francis at the church of San Damiano, toiling like a workman at the broken walls. How happy you and his mother must be! He is indeed becoming a good Christian."

Pietro Bernardone could not believe his ears. He sent Angelo out to see if it were true and Angelo returned with the news that it was. That was where Francis had been hiding! Bernardone fell into a great fury. His son had not been with Count Roland at all but had been wasting his time on a poor, broken-down church! Well, he would see to that! He rushed out of the shop, crying that he was going to take Francis away from a mad priest who had bewitched him.

Some of his friends followed, thinking that he might need help. By the time they neared San Damiano, they were quite a crowd. Francis could hear their cries as they came along the road. He became terribly frightened. Dropping the stone he was handling, he ran into the church. In two minutes he had slipped behind the painting and was in the hidden cellar.

He stood there, trembling, listening to the footsteps above. His father's angry voice rang out. Then he heard the priest saying mildly: "Yes, Francis was here, but I do not see him now."

At last, having searched everywhere and having failed to find his son, Bernardone was forced to give up and go away. After many hours Francis crept out of his hiding place. As he knelt before the crucifix, he did not feel very happy.

"I have wanted to be Your brave knight," he said, "but no knight was ever a greater coward."

As he prayed for courage, he made up his mind to go boldly to his father the next day and explain that he had entered the service of his Saviour.

By this time his clothes were ragged and stained. His hair had not been combed, and he was very thin and pale from lack of food. As he drew near his father's shop, praying that he would be a brave knight but with his knees trembling, some little boys saw him. They thought he had gone mad, for when people went mad in those days, that is the way they looked. The children ran after him, crying: "A madman! A madman!" They pelted him with stones, but Francis kept right on. When he entered the shop, the boys were still crying: "He is mad! He is mad!"

Pietro Bernardone cried out when he saw him. His face dark with anger, he would not listen to a word that Francis had to say. He ordered Angelo and Roberto to tie his arms and to take him home. His father followed, heaping curses upon his head. Arrived at the house, Bernardone unlocked the little dungeon and threw Francis into it with his arms still bound.

"There you shall stay," he cried, "until your senses return!"

The Lady Pica wept and begged her husband to release Francis. But that only made Bernardone angrier. Poor Maria and Lucia were so frightened by the noise that they did not dare come out of the kitchen. Angelo went over to the little dungeon and laughed at Francis through the bars.

"And this is my brother who was to become a fine knight and marry a great lady! What a fine knight *you* look like now! I'm sure that any great lady would be glad to have you!"

The poor Lady Pica could not help Francis because of her husband's anger. Francis stayed there all night, praying with all his heart that he would not desert his Lord. He could not stand up or move about; and now he again remembered the French teacher. Poor Master Jacques! At that time, he had thought it so funny that a man could not stand upright in the dungeon. What a little beast he had been!

Early in the morning before anyone else was awake, Maria tiptoed quietly to him. She carried a plate of food and set it down on the floor. Then, with a knife, she reached through the bars and cut the rope that tied him. She pushed the plate to him and, putting a finger to her lips, was gone. Francis ate the food hungrily and hid the plate behind him. Then he wound the rope around himself to look as though he were still tied. Later his father came to him and asked if he were ready to give up his folly. If so, he could return to the shop and all would be as it had been before. But Francis, thinking of the crucifix, only shook his head. Pietro Bernardone went away in a great rage.

Several days passed. Francis grew so stiff that he wondered if he would ever be able to walk again. At last one evening he heard his father say to the Lady Pica:

"Tomorrow I shall be gone all day on business in Spoleto."

Francis felt a pain in his heart. This was the sort of business that he used to do for his father, riding there on Raphael. What good times they had enjoyed and what fun it had been! But again he thought of the words that had come from the crucifix:

"Go, Francis, and repair My church, which you see is falling into ruin."

That was his business now. The other was finished.

The next morning, the Lady Pica waited only until her husband was out of sight. Then she ran and unlocked the little dungeon and set Francis free. In a few moments he had told her all that had happened. She embraced him and said:

"Go back, my son! Go back at once to San Damiano where the Lord has told you what you must do!"

"But my father?" asked Francis. "He will be very angry at *you* for setting me free!"

"Never mind," said the Lady Pica. "I will take care

of that. After all, you are my son, too. Later today I will send Maria over with some food for you and the poor Father Julio."

Francis hugged her and hurried back to San Damiano to resume his work on the church. When Bernardone returned that night, he was so angry to find that Francis had been set free that he struck the Lady Pica twice across the face. The next day he hurried over to the church to see his son. This time Francis did not hide but waited calmly for his father.

"If you will not return home and live as you should," shouted Bernardone, "then I command you to leave Assisi at once! The whole town is laughing at me for having a madman as a son!"

But Francis answered: "I will not obey your commands any longer. Now I am in the service of Christ and will do only as He commands me."

Then his father flew into a rage and cursed him.

"Think of all my money which you have wasted! Think of all my plans for you to become a knight and to marry a noble lady! Now you only disobey me! Think of the rolls of brocade and velvet which you stole from my shop! You must pay me back!"

"Come," said Francis, "here is your money." And he led his father into the church where the gold still rested on the window ledge. Bernardone fell upon it greedily and swept it into his purse.

From now on he was determined that Francis should be sent far away. He decided to appeal to the law. But

Sir Bernard of Quintavalle, the chief magistrate, advised
him that since Francis was now in the service of the
Church, only the Church could judge him. His father
went at once to the Bishop of Assisi and said:

"I wish to disinherit my son. I wish to do it publicly
—before the whole town—so that all may know that
I disown him!"

The kindly bishop, who had smiled at Francis on
that day when he had set forth to battle, was greatly
distressed. He liked Francis, yet he could not refuse
Bernardone's request. He sent word to the young man
that he must appear on a certain day in the public square
where the bishop's palace stood.

When Francis got there he was frightened at the great
crowd which had gathered. In his heart he prayed for
courage. As though in answer, once again the strange,
beautiful face he had first seen on the road near The
Three Angels, came before his eyes.

"Oh, fairest lady of them all," he begged, "tell me
who you are!"

But the face only smiled at him and vanished.

The bishop came out of his palace and stood on the
steps and Francis appeared before him. The crowd
gathered about them. Then came his angry father. The
bishop explained to Francis that his father wished to
disown him.

"And since," he went on, "you have said that you
wish to serve only the Church, it would be best if you
would say here, before all the people, that you now

give up all claim to your father's property. And you should return to him now anything you have which he has given you."

Francis said nothing, but to every one's surprise, walked quietly into the bishop's palace.

"Surely he is mad!" cried the crowd.

But in a moment a hush fell upon all, for there, before the bishop, stood Francis, clad in nothing but his long shirt. The clothes he had worn he carried in his hands. He turned to his father and laid them at his feet.

"I now return to you all I have that you have given me. And I declare before the bishop, and all the people, that I am no longer your son. I no longer shall call you father. For now I have but one Father; and that is He to Whom I pray: 'Our Father, Who art in heaven, hallowed be Thy Name.' "

Now Francis had nothing left in the world.

The crowd was very quiet. Bernardone, flushing, stooped down and gathered up the clothes. Francis stood there, shivering in the cold. The kind bishop, having pity on him, opened his own cloak and spread it about him. Just as he did so, Francis again saw before his eyes the face he loved. The vision smiled and her lips moved.

"You have wanted to know who I am," she whispered, "and you have earned the right. I am known to men as the Lady Poverty, but I am hard to win."

EIGHT

The Beggar and His Little Portion

A FEW days later in the early morning the lepers were eating breakfast in their little house among the trees when all at once they heard a voice singing on the road below. There was something about the voice that made them raise their heads to listen. It was clear and happy, and it was singing a song of love. They did not understand the words, but they knew it was a song of love, for the voice told them so.

Now as it came nearer the little boy on crutches hobbled over to peer out from the edge of the wood to see who was singing so beautifully. He called back to the others:

"It is—it looks like our new friend! But where is his horse?"

Then all the others came to look. They saw that indeed it was Francis, but quite a different Francis than the fine gentleman who had visited them before. Not only was his horse gone but also his rich clothing. He wore an old, worn-out cloak, but his slender face with its great dark eyes was the same.

Then he was in their midst, laughing and rumpling the hair of the little boy.

"Raphael sent you his kind regards," he said.

"But why aren't you riding him?" asked the boy.

"He is visiting a friend," explained Francis.

The lepers gave him a glad welcome and made him sit down and eat with them.

"My friends, I am no longer rich," explained Francis. "But you will see that I will be a better friend than ever. Like you, I now beg for my bread." He held out a corner of his tattered cloak. "Even this cloak was given to me in charity."

"Are you in love?" asked the boy. "It seemed to us that you were singing a song of love just now."

"Yes," said Francis. "I am in love with the fairest lady of them all!"

"And how is she called?" asked the lad.

"She is known as the Lady Poverty, and I was singing

that song to her, for I am trying very hard to win her."

"Oh, please," begged the boy, "sing it again!"

So Francis sang the song which the troubadours had taught him. He sang it in French—only by now he had made up new verses. They were all about the Lady Poverty, and how beautiful she was, but how very hard to find.

"Say the words in Italian," urged the boy.

Francis translated the words and all the lepers listened quietly.

"You have not found the Lady Poverty yet?" asked the boy.

"Oh, no; I am just beginning to search for her," explained Francis. "But now we must get to work! What about a bath and some fresh bandages?" From under his cloak he drew a bundle of clean rags.

There was a little stream that ran down the hillside, and soon Francis had bathed not only the boy, but the grown-ups, too, who could not bathe themselves. He put fresh bandages on them and it made them all feel much better. Then he went out to the roadside. In an hour he was back with a few coins and a half loaf of bread which he had begged.

"See what the sweet charity of Christ has given us!" he cried.

All the lepers were very happy. At last he said to them:

"I must leave you now but I will return again soon."

"Where are you going?" the boy asked.

"Back to my work."

"Well, give my love to Raphael!" cried the boy.

"I will when I see him," promised Francis.

Father Julio had not seen Francis since his father had disowned him. The old priest hurried out to greet him with open arms.

"My son! I am so glad you have returned!"

He had heard all about what had happened, and he felt very sorry for Francis.

"Do not be sad, Father, for I have never been as happy!" exclaimed his workman.

And indeed Father Julio, looking into his sparkling eyes and laughing face, knew that this must be true. Now the two set to work again, repairing the little church of San Damiano.

Soon all the holes on two sides of the church had been filled; but the third wall was still in a dreadful state. It would need a great many stones, and there were almost none left in the field. One morning Francis said to Father Julio:

"I will go into town and beg some stones."

"But how will you feel if you have to face your old friends, and perhaps even your family?" asked Father Julio.

"I don't know, but I mean to try, anyway."

In his tattered cloak he set off for town. He took up his stand in the market place. At first, no one paid any attention to him, for no one recognized him in his poor clothes. Francis began to speak to those who passed.

"Who will give me a stone to repair the poor church of San Damiano?" he asked.

Those who passed did not even look at him. Francis wanted to go right back to San Damiano. At last an elderly man heard him and stopped.

"I own the field just across from The Three Angels," he said, "and it is full of stones. I should be glad if you would carry some of them away."

Francis thanked him happily and was about to leave when the man stopped him.

"Are you not Francis, the younger son of the merchant Bernardone?"

"I *was* his son," answered Francis.

"I heard about what happened between you and your father. You have courage. You may take every stone in my field—and a blessing be upon you!"

Francis thanked him most gratefully and hurried away. Long before he reached the field, the whole town was buzzing with the talk that Francis Bernardone had been begging in the market place. His father was very angry and very ashamed but, since he had disowned his son, he could do nothing to stop him.

When Francis reached the field he set to work, making a pile of the stones. He was thinking that it was along this very road that he had first seen the face of the Lady Poverty; and of how she had changed his whole life. Then he heard a familiar voice and looked up to see Filippo standing there, grinning at him.

"Filippo!" cried Francis, grasping his hand.

"A change from the old days, eh?" asked Filippo, straightening the patch over his eye. "I hear you have become a church architect. Well, what better way could you spend your days? But you must get hungry there at the poor church?"

"Sometimes," said Francis, smiling.

"That should never be, Master Francis!" cried Filippo. "There is always plenty of food in the tavern. Come in now and have dinner with me!"

"Oh, thank you, Filippo, but I cannot. Father Julio is waiting, and I must carry these stones on my back to San Damiano before the sun sets."

"Well, I'm going to give you a basket of food to carry along too," said Filippo, hurrying into his tavern.

Now, with all the new stones and the good food, the work went faster. Very early every morning Father Julio celebrated Mass in the church. It now looked fresh and clean, with the lamp always burning and the candles glowing. One by one, all the people from the near-by farms, who had gone there in the old days, began coming back to Mass at San Damiano. Father Julio was very happy and so was Francis.

But as the winter drew on and it grew colder, fewer people came. One day when there was no more oil in the jug, and there were no more candles to light, Francis said:

"We need money, Father, and this evening I am going into town to beg it."

The sun had set, and the wind was cold and sharp, when Francis, in his ragged cloak, started up the hill. He decided he would walk through the town and look for a house where he might find several people together. But all the houses looked dark excepting one at the far end of a road. It was bright with many lights, but it was not until he came close to it that he recognized it. It was a palace of the Sciffi family, but not the one where he had enjoyed so many gay feasts in the past. Still, if he went in there, he might meet some of his old friends and he would be ashamed to beg before them. He started to turn away, but just then he caught a glimpse of the face he loved. The Lady Poverty was saying to him:

"But such are the hard paths you must travel to win me! 'Blessed are the poor in spirit'—don't you remember?"

He turned back and knocked at the great front door. As a servant opened it, the sound of music and laughter floated out, and he could see many people dancing and a fire blazing on the hearth. Francis blushed, but managed to ask:

"May I see your master for a moment?"

"The master is not here," said the man and was about to shut the door. Then he looked again at Francis. "You may come in and stand here. I will bring the master's son."

In a few moments he returned with a fair young man of smiling face, clad in a doublet of yellow velvet. Fran-

cis had never seen him before, but knew at once that he
was a Sciffi. He resembled Orlando, but yet was quite
different, too. Francis bowed.

"Your pardon, my lord, for intruding, but I am begging for the poor church of San Damiano. I hoped that
you might permit . . ."

"Of course," said the young man, smiling and drawing
out his purse. "Take this. Let us see if some others, too,
will not help the church."

He led Francis into the great room. Every one stopped
dancing and turned to look. It was as Francis had feared.
There were all his old friends, staring at him as though
he were a ghost—Orlando, Matteo, Armando, Antonio,
and Giorgio. They had been among those who had
thought that Francis had gone mad; and now they were
frightened at what he might do. There, also, stood the
Lady Ortolana and, at her side, a very beautiful young
girl who must, thought Francis, be the Lady Clare whom
he had not seen since she was a child. A great silence
had fallen on the company. Then Francis bowed and
spoke.

"I confess before all of you my sin of pride, for I
was ashamed to enter here and beg."

The Lady Ortolana at once came forward, smiling.

"Why, Rufino," she said to the young man at his side,
"this is Francis, our old friend! I'm sure that he wants
something for his church. Francis, I'm glad to see you!"
And she emptied her purse into his hand. Francis bowed
low and gave her his sunniest smile.

Now Orlando, Matteo, Armando, Antonio, and Giorgio saw that he was as charming as ever—that he did not act like a madman at all. They, too, crowded about him, laughing and happy to see him again.

"Even though you have deserted us, we still love you!" cried Orlando, as he, too, poured coins into the outstretched hand.

"It is for oil for the tabernacle lamp and for candles," explained Francis happily. "And may God bless all my dear friends for their charity!"

"Come," said Rufino. "As Orlando's cousin I cannot let his old friend go without offering him wine!"

Now there was something about Rufino that Francis had liked at once. He felt that he wanted to know him better.

"I thank you, my lord," he said, bowing, "but I cannot stay now. I hope that one day when you are riding near San Damiano you will stop."

"I will surely come," promised Rufino, smiling and nodding.

Again thanking them all, Francis took his leave and went out into the dark night, but his heart felt light and happy as he began the long, cold walk back to San Damiano. The pledge of friendship with the Sciffi family still held even though the ring had long since gone. And now he had coins in his purse to last San Damiano for many a day.

When he had gone, the young Lady Clare turned to her mother.

"Was not that the madman, Francis, who gave up a fortune? The one of whom every one has been talking? Why, I think he is not mad at all but very sensible!" . . .

Many other people now began to think as did the Lady Clare. As they watched Francis rebuilding the church, they almost always heard him singing. They saw him, too, in the market place and the public squares of Assisi, begging for stones and for bread, but always with a smile and often with a song. His mother, watching from afar, was satisfied that her son had indeed become "a good Christian."

He had made a simple robe for himself such as the hermits wore. It was of rough cloth, in one piece, and held at the waist with a leather strap. On his bare feet he wore sandals. He was happy except when he chanced to meet his father on the streets. Then it was terrible.

Pietro Bernardone, upon seeing his son, would break out into fury and utter loud curses against him. This often caused Francis to weep; but he did not run away.

At last in the year 1208, when Francis was twenty-six years old, the work on the church was finished. Francis went in to the altar and knelt before the crucifix.

"I have repaired Your church," he said. "Now, my Saviour, tell me what You wish me next to do, for I am forever Your knight!" . . .

That very afternoon as he walked down the hill to visit a poor man who was sick, he found the answer to his prayer. There, in a bit of forest, he came upon an ancient, ruined church. He had seen it before and knew that it was called Saint Mary of the Angels because long ago people had thought they had heard the singing of angels there. Now he entered it to pray. He saw that it was in as bad a state as had been San Damiano when he first went there. This time there was not even a priest about. The church belonged to the Benedictine monks who owned the great monastery high up on Mount Subasio which he had visited with Leo, but they had long ago abandoned it.

Now as Francis stood there, in all the gloom and decay, he, too, thought that he heard the singing of angels about him. What a lovely place this would be for prayer, hidden off in the forest and far from town! He went about, looking at all the broken walls and at the deserted altar. He saw exactly how he must clean and repair the church. Then he went outside and found the little house in which the monks had once lived. That, too, needed repair. He recalled that men in the town had often spoken of this place as the *Portiuncula*. At last he understood why. It was indeed a "little portion" of ground; and that was what the word *portiuncula* meant. Now he began here all the work that he had done at San Damiano.

One day early in May, Francis, standing in the church, thought how clean it looked. The altar was scrubbed and gleaming. It needed only a crucifix and candles; and, of course, the presence of Jesus in the tabernacle with a lamp burning before Him. He had begged a little money to supply all these things but One. If only

Jesus would come to dwell here again! But only a priest
could bring Him.

As he was thinking this, he suddenly heard a sound
at the open door. He turned and saw a monk standing
there.

"Good afternoon, Francis," said the monk. "I was
passing here on an errand for the monastery and saw
that our old church had taken on quite a new look."

"Welcome, Father!" exclaimed Francis. "Come in
and see."

The monk walked about looking at everything and
was greatly pleased.

Then Francis found the courage to ask:

"Father, if your abbot would consent, do you think
you might come here sometimes to celebrate Mass?"

"I will ask him certainly, for I should like very much
to bring our Lord here in the Blessed Sacrament. This
was always a holy place—Saint Mary of the Angels.
Now that you have restored it so well, Mass should
again be celebrated here."

Francis felt so sure the abbot would grant his request
that he hurried into town and bought a lamp, oil, and
candles. Early the next morning his friend appeared,
quite prepared to celebrate Mass. He placed our Lord
in the tabernacle and Francis lit the lamp and the candles.
There were fresh flowers on the altar. It was very beautiful there at the *Portiuncula* in the early morning, with
the song of the larks coming through the open windows.
When the monk turned to read the gospel, Francis stood

up. Then he heard these words which our Lord had
once spoken to His apostles:

"Go and preach, saying that the Kingdom of Heaven
is at hand. Heal the sick; cleanse the lepers. Freely you
have received; freely give. Provide neither gold nor
silver in your purses . . . Neither two coats, neither
shoes, nor yet staves. . . . And when you come into a
house, salute it; and if the house be worthy, let your
peace come upon it."

The words burned themselves into the heart of
Francis. He felt that our Lord was speaking directly to
him. Now he knew what he had next to do.

NINE

The Door of the Dead

AFTER the monk had gone back to his monastery, Francis went out into the forest. He had a little bread in his pocket, for he knew that the larks, whose song delighted him, would be hungry. He sat down under the trees and called up to them, and at once they were fluttering about him.

"You know," he confided to them, "that my Lord wants me to go and preach, but I'm not sure that I know how. I'm afraid that I was not much interested in school, so please be patient and listen, and let me practice on you."

The little birds stayed there at his feet, even when all the crumbs had vanished. Francis talked to them just as though they were people, and they listened quietly. When he had finished, he said:

"Thank you. And now it is time for you to sing and to praise God Who made you for His glory and for the delight of men."

At once the larks obeyed him, and Francis sang right along with them until the forest echoed with their music.

Early the next morning Francis walked up the hill to Assisi and began to preach in the market place.

Men stopped willingly to listen, for they knew him to be a holy man and a happy one while they themselves were sad. They wished to learn the secret of his gladness. Soon there were dozens of people gathered about him. So it went, day after day. He did not try to be learned, but he spoke to them from his heart, which was full of love for God and man.

One day two priests of the church of San Giorgio stood listening. When he had finished, they asked if he would come and speak from the pulpit of the church so that more people could hear him. That was how Francis began to speak in the churches; and first of all in his own San Giorgio which lay so near his old home.

One Sunday evening when he had just finished speaking there to a great crowd, someone touched his elbow. He turned to see his old friend, Sir Bernard of Quintavalle, the first magistrate of Assisi.

"Francis, all that you have just said is true. For a long time I have wanted to talk with you. Come home with me now and we shall dine together. I have much to ask you, so I hope you will spend the night at the palace, as it will be too late when we finish to return to the *Portiuncula*."

Francis was happy to agree. When they reached the great stone palace, Sir Bernard put his hand on the younger man's arm.

"This is the wall," he said, "which I saw you repair with your own hands to ease the burden of an old workman. Ever since then, I have been watching your deeds carefully."

"And did you, too, think that I had gone mad?" asked Francis, with a twinkle in his eye.

"On the contrary. I have come to think you the wisest man in Assisi."

After they had dined, the two talked late into the night. Sir Bernard explained that he had labored many years as magistrate to bring peace and justice to their city.

"But," he said, "we shall never have true justice until people change their ways. It is the poor, the *minores*, who suffer."

Now *minores* was the name by which the poor were

known, since they were minor folk, and of small importance compared to the rich, who were known as the *majores*.

"The *majores*, the nobles and the rich merchants like your father," went on Sir Bernard, "have everything their own way, but they crush the poor beneath their heels."

"I know," said Francis unhappily.

Francis spent most of that night in prayer, thinking of the poor *minores* whom he longed to help, but he could not do it all alone. He needed others to work with him. Early in the morning Sir Bernard tapped on his door.

"Francis," he said, "I have thought it all over during the night. I wish to be your companion and to help you in your work."

Francis was overjoyed at this answer to his prayer. Together they went out to a church which lay near by. When Mass was over, Francis drew Bernard to the Book of the Gospels, lying close to the altar.

"Let us pray," he said, "that God will direct us to open the book at a page where you may learn what He wishes of you."

After they had prayed, they opened the book. There they read these words which once, long before, our Lord had spoken to a rich man:

"If you will be perfect, go, and sell what you have, and give all to the poor."

Bernard knew at once that he must do just as Francis

had done. He must give up everything and become as
poor as the poor whom he wished to serve. The two
went to work, selling all the fine things which Bernard
owned. From these they collected a great heap of money.
Bernard gave it all to the poor and Francis helped him.
Now the great Sir Bernard of Quintavalle, clad in only
a hermit's robe and sandals, went down with Francis to
live at the Little Portion.

At once others followed him—Peter, a humble man
of Assisi who had often helped Francis; and Giles, from
a near-by farm, who had a merry heart like Francis. Like
him, Giles had always longed for great adventures such
as the troubadours sang of King Arthur and his knights.
They built shelters of trees, and Francis set them to
singing the praises of God and the love song to the
Lady Poverty. Because they seemed so happy, soon
other men came to join them. Some were rich, and these
did as Bernard had done, first giving all they had to
the poor. Others owned nothing, but they gave themselves to Francis and his work with a joyful heart.

At length they were twelve in all, living there at the
Little Portion and each day going out to help the sick
and the lepers. They worked in the fields with the
farmers and at any trade they knew to earn their bread.
Their needs were simple and they fed the poor first
before they fed themselves. When they could not earn
their bread, they begged for it—the knight at the side
of the shoemaker and the noble next to the farmer. In
the evening, after they had prayed in the church of

Saint Mary of the Angels, Francis would gather them together.

"We are knights of the Round Table," he would say, "and together we will do great things such as King Arthur's knights did long ago. We will bring justice and peace to the world. We will go into battle for a greater King than ever was King Arthur, for our King is God Himself. Each of us is a knight of the Great King and of the Lady Poverty. Each of us is also a *jongleur* for the King's pleasure. We are the *jongleurs* of God and must lift the hearts of others and make this sad world a merry one with our songs and our jests. We are both the knights and the *jongleurs* of God."

Well he remembered the day when, as a small boy, he had told his mother that when he grew up he wanted to be both a *jongleur* and a knight. It had all come true; but in quite a different way than any one had ever suspected. Finally Francis would say to his companions:

"We are all brothers here at the Little Portion. And this is why we have been called—that we may heal the wounded, and bind up the brokenhearted."

Then he sent the brothers out, two by two, to preach the word of God in all the villages and cities of Umbria and even farther off. He told them to greet every one with the prayer: "May the Lord give you peace!" At first people laughed at them because they were so poor; but gradually more and more began to listen. Francis decided that since they were knights of the Lady

Poverty, they would call themselves after the *minores* and would be known as the Brothers Minor. He wrote down a few simple rules by which they should live.

Ever since he had repaired San Damiano, he had been pledged to the service of the Church. Now that they were twelve in all, he decided that they should journey to Rome to ask the Pope to approve of all they were doing. The brothers walked all the way, singing and praying as they went and sleeping in the open fields.

Pope Innocent III listened in wonder while Francis explained that they owned nothing; that they had given everything away to the poor and that they were trying to copy the poverty which had been our Lord's while He lived upon earth.

"My son," said the Holy Father, "it is a hard path. Do you think that you and your brothers are strong enough to live by so harsh a rule?"

Francis was certain that they could. At last the Pope gave them his blessing and told them to continue. It was the year 1210, and Francis was twenty-eight years old. Happily they set off on the long walk back to Assisi. Just an hour before they reached it, they came upon a deserted little farmhouse near a stream which rolled down from the slopes of Mount Subasio.

"Let us stay here for a while," said Francis, "as no one seems to be living here. The Little Portion, where we lived before, really belongs to the Benedictine monks. Now that we are so many we have no right to stay there, but here we shall not be in anyone's way. Near by there are caves on the mountainside where each of us can go alone to pray."

So the twelve Brothers Minor moved into the little house at the place called Rivo Torto. Again they began preaching in Assisi and in all the towns about. Now that they had the Pope's approval, every one rushed to hear them and other young men came to Francis to ask if they, too, could work with him. Among them was Rufino, cousin of Orlando and of the Lady Clare, who had welcomed Francis that night at his palace when Francis had been ashamed to enter and beg. Rufino, as smiling as ever, had changed his velvet doublet for a rough robe and had given away all his money.

"From the moment I saw you, Francis, I knew that you would show me the way to God, so here I am— to do as you tell me!"

Francis welcomed him with open arms.

"You are another proof of the friendship of the Sciffi, which the Lady Ortolana pledged to me long ago. For a time, I feared that I had lost it!"

"Never," said Rufino. Then he added, laughing, "But I cannot promise that my cousin, Orlando, will follow me here!"

"No," agreed Francis, smiling, "but we shall never cease to pray for him."

One warm summer day when it was the hour for silent prayer, Francis had climbed a little way up the mountain to a certain cave where he could be alone and ask God to direct the Brothers Minor. They were now so many that they could not live much longer in the little farmhouse. Besides, they needed a chapel where Mass could be celebrated, and a priest to celebrate the Mass. Suddenly he thought of Leo. Whatever had happened to him? Surely he must be a priest by now! If only Leo would return and join the Brothers Minor!

Francis knelt for an hour on the cave's stony floor. When he came out, there was a figure sitting on a rock not far away. The man's back was turned to him, but his heart almost stood still. Could it be . . . ? Then suddenly the figure turned.

"Francis!"

"Leo!"

In a moment they had flung their arms about each other.

"They told me that I would find you at Rivo Torto," said Leo, "and one of the brothers there directed me here. I might have known that I would find you praying in a cave!"

Francis was so glad that he could hardly speak.

"God is so good," he kept saying over and over; "God is so good!"

"I have served all these years as a priest in Bologna," explained Leo, "but when word reached there of the work you were doing, I begged permission to join you."

"You will become a Brother Minor?" asked Francis joyfully.

"If you will take me."

"From this moment you are Brother Leo!" cried Francis.

"Do you remember one day," asked Francis as they walked down the mountainside, "when I told you that, if I were to go into business, you could be my secretary and do all my writing?"

"Yes," said Leo. "That was when we were walking away from another cave."

"Well," said Francis with a gay laugh, "I'm not exactly a man of business, but I'm one who needs a secretary. And so you shall be my secretary after all!"

"Is that so?" smiled Leo. "But you've forgotten the rest of it. I said that when I became a priest you would have to come to me in confession, and that then I could give you a very heavy penance!"

"It is a bargain!" cried Francis.

Of all the happy brothers who had come to join him it seemed that Leo was the happiest of all. He fell into their way of life at once—as though it had been made for him.

One morning not much later they all awoke to the sound of a driving rain. They were wondering how they could go about their work when they heard a scuffle at the door. Before they knew it, it was pushed open from the outside and in walked a big donkey with a farmer at his heels, driving the beast before him.

"Get in!" he said to the donkey. "Walk right in! You and I have been looking for a home, and this will do us quite well."

As the donkey walked in, Francis made them all laugh by saying: "Ah! a new brother has come to join us! Welcome, Brother Jackass!" And he gave him a friendly pat. The donkey brayed in answer, which made every one laugh all the harder.

The donkey made himself perfectly at home, as did his master. Francis could not tell them to leave as he did not own the place. But he knew that now the Brothers Minor must find another home. So when the rain had stopped, he and Leo walked up the mountain to the Benedictine monastery. There Leo waited while Francis went in and talked with the abbot, who still wore the great ring on his finger and the heavy gold chain about his neck. He knew all about the good work that Francis had done, and exclaimed:

"Why, if the Brothers Minor need a home, I will give them the Little Portion! Did you not restore the church for us? No one is using it now. We shall be very happy if the brothers will live there and have Mass celebrated for all the people near by."

"How long, my lord, may we stay?" asked Francis.

"Forever!" laughed the abbot.

Francis, in much gratitude, kissed his ring. Then he and Leo went off, very happy that the brothers now had both a church and a home.

People now came from far and wide to Assisi to hear Francis preach. Because of the crowds, he had been asked to preach in the great cathedral of San Rufino, whose bells he had once set to ringing in the dead of night to startle the poor *podesta*. How far away all that now seemed! Among those who came to hear him every Sunday were the Lady Ortolana and her daughter, the Lady Clare.

Clare, with her long golden hair and big brown eyes, had grown more beautiful every day. Her father, the Lord Faverone, had early begun to make plans for her marriage to some rich and noble knight. But Clare always made an excuse. Indeed, there were many knights who wished to marry her, for she was not only beautiful and good, but she was also very rich. When her sister Agnes, who was three years younger than Clare, and their cousin Pacifica, who lived with them, questioned her, Clare would always say:

"I shall never marry. I have other plans; you will see!"

Now in the palace of the Sciffi there was a great dark oaken door which no one ever opened. In fact, no one even liked to pass it. When the maids had to go that way, they ran by in fear and turned their faces away. Never would they pass it at night, for the hall was but dimly lighted. It was called the Door of the Dead and was opened only when some one in the palace had died. Through it, the dead were carried to their burial. The door was never used for anything else.

One night at dinner in the early spring, the Lord Faverone said to Clare:

"Daughter, you are now eighteen and it is time that you were married. I will hear of no more delays. I have invited a fine knight of Perugia, who is young, handsome, and rich, to stay with us here at the palace. He will come right after Easter. He wishes to marry you and my wish also is that you should marry him."

The smile faded from Clare's face and she went very pale. Easter! Why Easter of the year 1212 was only two weeks away!

"But, Father . . . "

"Enough!" cried her father. "Those are my wishes and you shall obey them."

Clare looked at her mother. While the Lady Ortolana seemed to be sad, yet she nodded to Clare as though to say, "You must do what your father asks!"

That night when Clare was alone in her room, she wept bitterly and prayed. Early the next morning before anyone was awake she went out to the stables and saddled her horse. A sleepy maid, looking out from a window, saw her take the road which led toward the plain. She thought no more of it because Clare returned an hour or two later and was there as the family gathered for breakfast.

Later that morning, when Pacifica and Agnes went to look for Clare, they searched the palace in vain. Finally Agnes said:

"We have looked everywhere. There is left only the long, dark hall where stands the Door of the Dead. But surely she could not be there!"

"Let us go and see," said Pacifica, who was older. "I'm not afraid; are you?"

"Oh, no," replied Agnes bravely, but with trembling knees.

Off the two went and, sure enough, there stood Clare

before the big, dark door. She was trying to open it.

"There," she said, "it isn't so hard to open after all. See, I've already moved it!"

Slowly the great door swung wide. Beyond it all they could see was a road overgrown with grass and the open fields.

"But why did you wish to open it?" asked the others, quite puzzled.

"Oh, I was just curious," answered Clare.

During the days that followed, Clare seemed strangely silent. The Lady Ortolana felt sure it was the thought of the marriage which troubled her. She tried her best to comfort her daughter. It happened that the following Sunday was Palm Sunday, and so she said to Clare:

"Come, dear; we shall go together to the cathedral to hear the holy Francis preach. Surely that will make you feel better!"

For the first time in days her daughter began to smile again. But all through the service it seemed to her mother that Clare was held fast as though in a dream. Later that day, Clare took a long walk with Pacifica and Agnes. When the three returned they seemed very silent and not at all like the laughing girls that every one in the palace knew. That night, long after every one had gone to bed, and when all was dark and still, Clare tapped softly at Pacifica's door. She had changed her rich golden gown for a long veil and a dark robe and held a candle in her hand.

"Come," she whispered, "it is time!"

Pacifica, also in a dark robe, followed Clare as she led the way on tiptoe down the great stone stairway and out into the dark hall of the Door of the Dead. Pacifica was terribly frightened. Together they opened the heavy door.

"We cannot leave by any other way," whispered Clare, "for one of the guards would surely see us!"

They were afraid as they passed through the door and clung to each other, looking back fearfully over their shoulders. Thick dust dropped down upon them, and the spiders ran in every direction. But once out in the open, they had no trouble in quietly getting their horses from the stable.

Meantime, down at the Little Portion, Francis and the brothers made ready to welcome them. It had been to Francis that Clare had gone on that early morning more than a week before. Together they had planned her escape. Clare had told Francis that she would never marry; that with all her heart she wanted only to serve God and the poor, as Francis was doing. And she begged him to help her.

On this night all the brothers lit torches and went out to stand along the way to meet Clare and Pacifica. Brother Bernard was there, and Brother Peter, and Brother Giles, Brother Rufino and Brother Leo. When they saw them coming, the brothers broke into song. Brother Rufino, Clare's own cousin, helped her down from her horse. Francis led all of them into the church of Saint Mary of the Angels. Once again it seemed to

him that he heard the angels singing. The altar was beautiful with candlelight and flowers. Then when all had
sung and prayed, Clare stood before the altar and took
off her veil. Her long hair tumbled down about her
waist and shone like gold in the candlelight.

Francis knelt and prayed. Then, while every one
looked on, he touched with reverence the beautiful hair
and slowly cut it off. Clare stood with her hands folded
in prayer as the long tresses fell to her feet. Then Francis
gently covered her head with the veil and she stood
there—the beautiful young girl suddenly transformed
into a nun. Francis did the same for Pacifica. It was a
scene that none of the brothers would ever forget. As
for Clare, she felt happier than she had ever felt in her
whole life. . . .

While all this was happening, back in Assisi the palace
of the Sciffi was in an uproar. Day had broken, and
someone had found the Door of the Dead swinging wide.
Clare was missing. The Lord Faverone, roused from
sleep, was beside himself with fear and anger. The Lady
Ortolana, weeping, could not get young Agnes to tell
her anything. Agnes would have died rather than betray
Clare. Now the Lord Faverone called all his knights
and his kinsmen together.

"Go out and find her!" he roared. "Search through
all Assisi and all the countryside. Bring her back to me—
that she may be fitly punished! And kill any man who
dares to stand in your way!"

TEN

The Sultan and His Golden Tent

When Francis had covered Clare's head with the dark veil, he and the brothers guided the two cousins through the night to a convent which lay some distance from the Little Portion. The abbess received the girls gladly and promised to shelter them. Francis explained that soon he would find a convent of their own for them, for Clare had other friends who wished to join her in serving the poor.

Then the brothers started back to the Little Portion.

It was quite a long walk and, when they got there, the sun had already risen.

"You may be sure, my brothers," said Francis, "that the Lady Clare's father, the Lord Faverone, will send his knights here to search for her."

"Well, then," said Rufino, "I will go out to meet them, for I, too, am a Sciffi and kinsman to the Lord Faverone. They will learn from me that she has come to no harm."

Francis thanked him and said:

"After you have met them, please lead them to me that I may tell them where the Lady Clare is to be found."

"Oh, no!" cried the others. "They would surely take her away from the convent!"

"I think not," said Francis smiling.

And so it came about. Rufino could hear the thunder of the horses' hoofs as they pounded toward the Little Portion. His kinsmen stormed and even cursed him; but when he led them to Francis who greeted them calmly, they fell silent and ashamed.

"Tell the Lord Faverone," said Francis, "that his daughter can be found at the convent of the good nuns."

They galloped back to the palace with the news.

"It's well that he told you," growled Faverone. "Otherwise I should have expected you to run him through with your swords!"

The knights said nothing, but each knew in his heart that he could not have killed "the Little Poor Man," as every one now called Francis.

"Come, we will ride at once to the convent!" cried Faverone. Then he turned to his wife. "Do not worry," he said, "for we shall have Clare back here again before noon!"

"Oh, I hope not!" whispered young Agnes to her mother.

The Lady Ortolana looked at her daughter in amazement as the horsemen clattered out of the courtyard.

Francis had sent word to Clare to be prepared. When her father thundered at the convent gate with all his knights behind him, the gentle nun who opened it said that they would find the Lady Clare in the chapel. Roughly they strode through the halls and flung open the door. There knelt Clare before the altar. As her father advanced she rose to face him but put one hand on the altar to steady herself.

"What nonsense is this?" cried Faverone. "We have come to carry you home!"

Clare faced her father quietly.

"I am not coming," she said.

Then the Lord Faverone stormed and fumed as she repeated again and again that she had now pledged her life to God and the poor. Nothing he could say would move her. At last, in despair, he tried to pull her away, but she only clung to the altar all the harder. Finally, with tears in his eyes, her father turned and went down the aisle alone with bowed head. Never before had his lovely daughter disobeyed him. Was this how she was to end? Shut up in a convent, with all the world waiting to give her happiness! Ah, well, perhaps she would get over this madness. He would send her mother to see her.

But before this could happen, another strange event befell the noble family of the Sciffi. One dark night the young Agnes, scarcely fifteen, also disappeared from the palace. They guessed at once where she had gone; and this time her father's anger knew no bounds. That this mere *child* should also run away from home! She had been bewitched by her sister. Off the Lord Faverone rode again with all his knights behind him. This time there was a terrible scene.

They clattered into the convent and tore Agnes away from her sister's side. They carried her out the door and down the path. Poor little Agnes wept and called out to Clare:

"Oh, sister, sister! Save me, save me!"

Clare had dropped to her knees in prayer. She begged God with all her heart to set Agnes free. Then a strange thing happened. The slender young girl, who, to these strong men, seemed to weigh no more than a feather, suddenly grew as heavy as a great block of marble. They staggered to their knees and fell under the weight. Agnes rolled off into the bushes. Terrified at this strange happening, the knights took to their heels, crying, "It is a sign from God! Surely He wishes her to remain in the convent!" The Lord Faverone's wrath was terrible, but he could not defy a Power stronger than his.

The news was not long in reaching Francis and his brothers at the Little Portion, where they had been praying constantly for Clare and her sister. They all rejoiced—especially Rufino—who said:

"You see, Brother Francis, in spite of all Faverone's anger you still have the friendship of the Sciffi! For behold, there are now four of us who have given up everything to follow you: Clare, Pacifica, Agnes, and me—Rufino—the least of your brothers."

Francis smiled and said:

"The Good God is so good!"

Now he set about finding a convent for Clare and the others, for by this time many friends of theirs had come to him, wishing to do as they had done. They would give all they owned to the poor; they would pray and work with Clare, as Francis might direct. Again he went to the kind Benedictine abbot on the mountain.

"Well, Francis," he said, "if you need a convent for these new nuns and their holy work, I will give you the church and house of San Damiano. You also repaired these with your own hands, as you did the Little Portion. As you know, our good friend Father Julio is dead and will no longer need them."

Francis almost danced down the mountainside he was so filled with joy. He and all the brothers, singing as they went, escorted Clare, Pacifica, and Agnes to their new convent. It was the little house he had once shared with Father Julio. Clare's friends joined them there. And in the church of San Damiano, before the crucifix whose Christ had once spoken to Francis, Agnes and the others received their veils. So began the Order of the Poor Ladies, as they called themselves. Francis said to them:

"The brothers and I will bring you all your food. We will earn it by our labor, or beg it in the name of the sweet Christ."

And Clare answered:

"In return, we shall always pray for you and your work. We will farm the fields and feed the poor. We will care for the sick. We will spin and make linen for the poor churches."

The people of Assisi were much pleased with the Poor Ladies who did not spare themselves in doing good. When Francis and his brothers went off to preach in distant places, he always left some friars (as the brothers were also called) to watch over Clare and her sisters. From her tiny flower garden on the terrace, Clare could look down at the Little Portion lying in the distance and know that the brothers would always protect her convent.

One day when Francis was off on a journey with Leo and Rufino, a tall man famous for his bravery stopped to hear him preach. At the end he saluted Francis with great courtesy and at once begged to join his company. He was dressed in the fine clothing of a knight, which Francis himself had once dreamed of wearing. Francis welcomed him happily and said:

"For long you have worn the belt, the sword, and the spurs of a knight of this world. Come with me and I will make you a knight of Christ!"

At once the knight took off his sword and spurs and laid them at the feet of Francis. Then he put on the rough robe of the friars. That was how Sir Angelo Tancredi became Brother Angelo. Every one liked him for his courtesy, and he and Leo and Rufino became very good friends. Soon people called them the Three Companions, for they worked much together and were very loyal to Francis.

Sometimes his journeys took Francis into the mountains near Chiusi. Then he always stopped to see his old friend, Count Roland and, of course, Raphael. Raphael was much older now, led an easy life in a big green pasture and slept in a fine stable. He always knew his old master when he came and would run to meet him, tossing his mane into the air. Francis would stroke his nose, feed him a honey cake, and call him "Brother Raphael." Then he would sit down in the pasture and the two would have long talks, just as in the old days.

As they talked, Francis would often look up at the beautiful Mount of La Verna, towering into the blue sky above the Count's castle. He still longed to climb it, for he knew that on those misty heights he would find quiet places to pray—far away from the world and very close to God. One day when he was looking up at it, Count Roland who was standing near, said:

"I would like to make you a present, Francis, so I will give you the Mount of La Verna for your own."

Francis could hardly believe his ears. The mountain was just what he wanted. He thanked his friend most gratefully.

In those days Leo went with Francis on all his journeys so that he could take down in writing the letters which Francis now had to send far and wide. So many others had come to join them that directing the work of the Brothers Minor kept him very busy. By this time the friars were scattered over many parts of Europe.

Among the new brothers was Juniper, who was a delight to all. A shoemaker by trade, he earned his bread by mending shoes, and he won all hearts with his jokes and merrymaking. The Lady Clare called him "God's *jongleur*," for not only could he always make every one laugh, but he was also very holy. He would go off in his rough robe but almost always came back without it, for he could never resist any beggar who might ask him for it. The friars had a hard time of it, keeping a robe on Brother Juniper's back.

The news of his holiness soon spread all over Italy. Juniper did not like this. Once, when Francis sent him on a mission to Rome, some pious ladies heard that the holy man was drawing near and went out to meet him. Juniper saw them coming and wanted to run, but there was no place to hide. Just then he happened to see some children playing on a seesaw. He ran up and jumped right on the seesaw with them. The children squealed with delight to find this strange friar riding up and down with them, his long legs dangling and his robe flying in the breeze. The ladies were horrified to see how a holy man could behave. Why, he was on his way to visit the Pope himself! Shocking! They turned their backs on him and went away—and that was exactly what Juniper wanted.

Never was there such a mixed gathering of men as were the early Brothers Minor. They were farmers and knights; shoemakers and lawyers; poor peasants and those who had been rich nobles. One early morning when they had all come back to the Little Portion, after spending the night in taking care of the lepers and tending the sick, Francis looked at them and said to himself:

"There is every sort of man here save one, but the company is not complete, for as yet we have no brigands. It would be nice if our Lord would let me convert a few brigands."

Soon he happened to glance down the road and saw a familiar figure coming toward him. He could never mistake that big frame and that black patch over one eye. It was Filippo himself from The Three Angels.

"Master Francis," he cried with a broad grin, "I have sold the tavern and given the money to the poor; and now I am here to do as you tell me!"

Francis laughed with joy.

"Only just now I was praying for a brigand! You haven't been a brigand for a long time, good Filippo, but you must *know* some brigands whom we can convert!"

The other assured him that he did. Now it became Brother Filippo's work to seek out the brigands. Soon there were three nice brigands turned into brothers and living a happy, honest life down at the Little Portion.

In fact, all the world around Assisi and in most of Italy had become happier because Francis had taught men to stop thinking about themselves and to think about others —above all, about God.

Because Francis loved God so much, he was not content with having given up everything in the world for Him. "There is one thing more that I have not given and that is my life," he said to himself. "Now if I could only lay down my life for Him, I would be much happier."

One day he called Leo to him.

"Do you remember," he asked, "how once long ago I told you that some day I hoped to follow a Crusade to the Holy Land? Well, Brother Leo, I am off to join a Crusade!"

"But why?" asked Leo unhappily. "You have plenty of work to do right here!"

"I want to lay down my life for Christ, and I see no other way that I can be killed for Him, except in a Crusade. Before the Saracens kill me, I hope that our Lord will let me make many converts."

Just at that time an army of Crusaders was besieging the city of Damietta in Egypt. The Saracens were blocking their way to the Holy Land, the land of Christ which the Crusaders wanted to win from the infidels. Francis, with some of his brothers, set out to join them. His boyhood dream was coming true; he was to fight in a Crusade after all. It would not be as a fine knight in splendid armor, but rather as a poor friar.

When he arrived at Damietta, he went all about the

Christian camp, talking everywhere of God. Soon there were dozens of knights and soldiers who wanted to give all they had to the poor and follow Francis. He was happy about this; but now it was time, he thought, to make converts among the Saracens, too, and to die for his Lord.

Early one morning he left the safety of the Christian camp and started across the wide open space that lay between it and the Saracen army. A friar named Brother Illuminato trotted along at his side although terribly frightened. Arrows were flying through the air in every direction. The great Duke Leopold of Austria, who was in command of the Christian army, looked out from his tent and saw Francis hurrying right into the arms of the enemy. He turned to his generals and asked:

"Who is that madman?"

"It's the holy friar Francis, from Italy, who is going over to convert the Saracens," they answered.

" I only wish that I had ten men as brave as that friar!" exclaimed the Duke. "Then we would win this Crusade."

Now the Saracen army was commanded by a great and powerful Sultan.

"I must somehow get to see the Sultan himself," said Francis to his companion as they hurried along.

"Oh, no, Father Francis!" protested Illuminato, as he dodged a flying arrow, "for he would surely kill us— if these arrows don't do so first!"

"What a wonderful death!" cried Francis, starting to run toward the enemy lines. "If he should kill us, think how many of his people would be converted to Christianity!"

"T-t-t-true," stuttered the poor brother, his knees quaking under him and all out of breath from trying to keep up with Francis.

Just then they were surrounded by a group of fierce, shrieking Saracens, all waving their curved swords at them. Francis held up his hand and said politely:

"I'll be happy to have you kill me; but first please let me see your Sultan. I have an important message for him."

The soldiers paused. Perhaps it was a message of surrender from the Christian army. Instead of killing Francis and Illuminato they led them to the center of the camp where there stood a magnificent tent all made of cloth of gold. It glittered in the sunshine, and the wind blew out the red banners which fluttered high from every corner. Inside, the Sultan, wearing a turban sparkling with jewels, sat on a fine throne. About him stood a guard of fierce soldiers and some of his priests. Brother Illuminato could not stop the shaking of his knees, but Francis at once began to speak to the Sultan about Christ.

Now the Sultan could be very cruel to Christians. In fact, he had promised a large gold piece to any soldier who would bring him the head of a Crusader. But the more he looked at Francis, the better he liked him.

"How do I know that your Christ is more powerful than our Mohammed?" he asked pleasantly.

Francis was disappointed to find so pleasant a Sultan. He feared he would be too pleasant to kill him. So he began to talk all the more about Christ and to say how little he thought of the Sultan's Mohammed.

"I will prove to you that Christ is God!" he cried. "Just order a great fire to be made. I will walk right into it with one of your own priests. Then you will see which is the true religion!" He looked at the Sultan's chief priest standing close to the throne.

The Sultan seemed amused.

"I don't believe that any of my priests will accept your challenge," he said, smiling. And, indeed, at this point the chief priest turned pale and hurriedly left the tent.

"Well, then," said Francis, "I will walk into the fire alone, for I want nothing better than to die for Christ and so prove to you that He is God!"

"Come, come," said the Sultan, "you are too nice a fellow to die. Sit down here near me and have some of these sugared dates. This honeyed wine is excellent, too," he said, as he poured out a cup for Francis.

Francis was so disappointed that he could have wept, but he had to sit down and talk with the Sultan. Soon they became great friends.

"If you will stay here with me," said the Sultan, "I will make you rich and you shall have everything you desire."

In vain did Francis try to explain about the Lady Poverty. The Sultan simply could not understand. At last Francis had to give up and say that he and Brother Illuminato must be getting back to the Christian camp. The Sultan was sorry to see them go but gave them a guard all the way. He wanted to give Francis many beautiful gifts; however, the Little Poor Man would accept only one big brass horn. He knew that he could use it later when calling people to come to hear a sermon.

After he got back to the Christian camp he kept asking our Lord:

"Why did You not let me die for You there among the Saracens? My heart is sad because that Sultan was so very pleasant."

He was just thinking that it was now time to get back to Assisi and take with him all the new Brothers Minor whom he had converted, when a messenger found him. He had come all the way from Italy, and the poor brother was breathless with haste.

"Come home; come home quickly, Father Francis!" he cried. "The friars need you, for there is great trouble at the Little Portion!"

ELEVEN

The Dawn of Holy Cross Day

ON THE journey home across the sea Francis was
worried about his brothers. The messenger could not
tell him much, except that the Three Companions—Leo,
Angelo, and Rufino—had sent word to hasten. Brother
Bernard, Brother Giles, and Brother Juniper, too,
wanted Francis to know how much he was needed.

From the Little Portion Leo was the first to see the
travelers coming down the road. With a happy shout
he ran forth to meet them. Soon they were all clustered

about Francis, and once again the forest resounded with
their song. Francis gathered only his first friars about
him for a long talk.

"The new brothers have brought a change," explained
Leo. "Many think that our life is too hard with poverty."

"Some think that we should *own* our houses and
monasteries and not just borrow them, or always be looking to someone to give them to us," went on Giles in-
dignantly. "They think that we should own money and
have the right to buy and sell land!"

Juniper looked very unhappy.

"Please don't change anything, Father Francis!" he
begged.

"I was gone too long," said Francis gently. "I am
sorry. But now lift up your hearts, for I shall call together a great meeting of all the friars. Even those in
faraway countries shall come here to the Little Portion.
Then we will make everything clear again: that we
follow the Lady Poverty, and her alone." He turned to
Leo:

"And how has our sister, Clare, fared in all this
trouble?"

"They have wanted her to change her rules also,"
answered Leo. "They have told her that she and her
nuns cannot lead so hard a life."

"But the Lady Clare refused to listen!" broke in
Juniper happily.

Francis smiled and said:

"The Lady Clare long ago took the Lady Poverty as her own sister."

With Brother Leo he walked up the hill to see her and to thank her for remaining faithful to his ideas. They found Clare in her garden which now was bright with summer flowers. She was so glad to see Francis that she knelt at his feet and kissed the hem of his robe.

Then Francis went into the church of San Damiano to pray long before the crucifix whose words he had tried so carefully to obey. When he came out, he felt that from now on he should give more time to prayer alone; that he should let others direct the large army of brothers. All this he made clear to the friars who came from far and wide to attend the meeting. Again and again he reminded them of their pledge to the Lady Poverty. But now the army was so vast that it was necessary to make new rules, which Francis agreed to write.

Not long after the meeting, the Pope made the Brothers Minor a true order of the Church. It was the year 1220, and Francis was now thirty-eight years old. Already he had founded two orders, the Order of Friars Minor, or his First Order, and the Order of the Poor Ladies, or his Second Order. Between praying and preaching, his days were now very busy.

One bright sunny morning when he had journeyed to a near-by town to preach on the steps of a church, the swallows which clustered under its roof gave him a noisy welcome. There seemed to be hundreds of them, all chirping and chattering at once. A large crowd of people had gathered to hear the Little Poor Man of Assisi, but when he opened his mouth to speak, the swallows set up such a clamor that he could not be heard. Francis raised his head to the noisy swarm and said:

"My little sisters, the swallows, it is now time for me to speak because you have been saying quite enough all this time! Now listen to the word of God and be quiet!"

At once the swallows stopped chattering and were silent. They sat perched above him and did not move, listening to every word he said. The men and women of the town were amazed to see how even the birds obeyed him. And when he had finished his beautiful sermon they cried out:

"Tell us how we, too, may follow you! We cannot become friars or nuns because we are married and have children to care for. But even so, can we not follow your way of life?"

Francis told them how they could serve the poor, take care of the sick, pray, and yet remain as they were in the world. He gave them rules, and all the people were happy to follow them. Soon there were groups of men and women doing the same thing in many cities of Italy. Francis was happy and called these good people who were neither friars nor nuns his Third Order.

About this time the people of a town named Gubbio were in great trouble. A thick forest lay at the edge of the town, and in the forest there lived a very fierce wolf. He was so big and strong that it seemed he could never get enough to eat. He began running into the town at night and eating up all the chickens. It was no good trying to lock them up. The wolf was so strong that he could break down almost any door. Finally, when he had eaten up all the chickens he began stealing the children and eating them too. Brave men of the city went out into the forest to hunt him and kill him, but they never came back. The people wept, prayed, and lived in constant fear. Suddenly someone thought of Francis.

"It is said that this holy man of Assisi has a wonderful way with animals and all creatures. Let us send to him and beg him to come to us and rid us of the Wolf of Gubbio!"

The message reached Francis at the Little Portion and at once he set out.

"If only you had a dagger or something!" exclaimed Leo, who was very anxious about him.

"I will not need it, Brother Leo," smiled Francis.

When he arrived at Gubbio, the people of the town met him with both hope and fear. Would the wolf kill him? Then all Italy would be furious at them, for Brother Francis was greatly beloved. But Francis was not at all frightened.

"Show me where I may find my brother, the Wolf," he said.

They took him up on the walls of the city, and pointed down to a spot in the forest, saying:

"We will stay here and watch you." No one dared to go with him.

Even as they spoke they could see the wolf sticking his nose out from among the trees. He was just waiting for the dark to come so he could bound over the walls and carry off another child.

Breathlessly the people now watched Francis as he went toward the forest. He had gone only a few steps when the great wolf bounded out and, with flashing teeth, made straight for him. The women screamed and covered their eyes. But the men, shaking with terror, suddenly saw an amazing thing. Just as the wolf, with open jaws, was about to leap upon the Little Poor Man and devour him, Francis raised his hand and made the sign of the cross. At once the wolf stopped and crouched on the ground. Then everyone could hear Francis say:

"Come here, Brother Wolf!"

It was very strange indeed to see the fierce animal now trot forward like a friendly puppy and curl right up at the feet of Francis. Francis stooped and patted him on the head.

"In the name of the sweet Christ I forbid you from now on to be evil," he said. "You know, Brother Wolf, I have been sorry to hear of the shocking way you have behaved to the people of Gubbio. It is said that you have even killed their little children. You deserve to be punished, but I would much rather have you and the people of this town become good friends."

The wolf seemed to understand perfectly. He looked up at Francis and wagged his big, bushy tail.

"Now, Brother Wolf, if you will promise to behave, I will promise in return that you will always have plenty to eat—for the rest of your life! I know that it has been hunger which has driven you to such crimes."

The wolf got up and rubbed himself against the robe of Francis.

"Will you promise to be a good wolf from now on?"

At that moment every one saw the most wonderful thing of all, for the wolf sat down and stretched out his big right paw to Francis. Francis took it in his hand and shook it. Then and there he and the wolf reached their honorable bargain. The two now started back to Gubbio with the wolf trotting happily along at the side of Francis. When they reached the market place, all the people ran to see them. Francis said to them:

"My brother, the Wolf here, has sworn never again to be evil if you, on your part, will swear that for the rest of his life he shall never go hungry."

The people then cried with a loud voice that they would always take good care of the wolf. And Brother Wolf was so pleased that he wagged his great tail back and forth, and shook his big ears, and again stretched out his right paw to Francis. Francis held it a long time, and so the agreement was sealed.

From that day onward, every one in Gubbio was very good to the wolf. They gave him a warm place to sleep right in the town and good food to eat every day. He went in and out among the children and played with them; and every one came to love Brother Wolf. At last he died of old age and the people wept. They buried him in an honorable place and even built a church over the spot. They wanted to keep him near them always, for not only had he been a good friend, but also he reminded them of Francis who had saved them. . . .

Francis had a great love for the Christ Child and the feast of Christmas, so, when Christmas of the year 1223 drew near, he resolved to honor it in quite a new way. He journeyed to the town of Greccio which was perched on a mountainside thick with evergreen trees.

When Christmas Eve came, and it was nearing midnight, people could see the friars coming up the mountain from every direction with lighted torches in their hands. All the people followed until they reached a place where, on a rocky ledge, an altar had been made. The stars shone down through the trees upon a real manger filled with hay. There stood a real ox and a real donkey at its side.

Mass was celebrated, and Francis read the Gospel as he stood before the manger. He spoke about the birth of the Great King in poverty and then he bent over the manger in prayer. Many people said that suddenly they seemed to see a beautiful Child lying there and smiling up at Francis. It was the first time that anyone had ever thought of reminding the world of the first Christmas in this special way. From that time forward, there has always been a crib near the altar of all churches everywhere at Christmastide.

Ever since Francis had gone on the Crusade, he had not been well. It was his spirit which carried him along, but sometimes the spirit went so fast that it was hard for his body to keep up with it. When his body asked for food, he would say to it: "Keep quiet. It is time to pray!" And when his body asked for sleep, he said: "Stop crying. We must go out to nurse the lepers!" His body seemed very stubborn, trying to keep him from all the things he wanted to do for his Lord, and so he began to call it "Brother Jackass." He fed Brother Jackass very poorly. Leo watched him anxiously and was worried.

One August morning when Francis was about forty-two years old, he called Leo to him and said:

"Let us journey to our beloved mountain of La Verna and spend forty days there in prayer. We will take Angelo and Rufino with us, and Brother Illuminato, who bravely went with me to see the Sultan. We will also take Brother Masseo, whom people love because he speaks well and is handsome. He will see that we shall get what bread we may need."

Leo was glad to be invited, for indeed Francis looked so ill these days that Leo did not like him to go anywhere alone. When they reached La Verna and began the long climb upward, Francis felt very happy. Near the top of the mountain, he found a cave where he could be quite alone. In order to reach it, they had to make a bridge of logs across a wide chasm. Francis told Leo that he must not cross the bridge except once a day to bring him a little food and water. Leo and the others found caves for themselves on the other side, but Leo continued to worry about Francis.

"What if he should die?" he thought. "Then I would be left living and I would have nothing of his to keep. I wish he would write me a letter, or something before he dies, that I could always keep! But he never writes any letters himself. It is I who have been doing that for him all these years."

Leo looked at the little inkpot and the paper and pen he had carefully brought with him—just in case Francis might wish to dictate a letter. He could not very well ask Francis to dictate a letter to *him!* That would look silly; and, besides, he did not wish Francis to guess that he was worried about him.

One day, as he was thinking these things and was greatly troubled, he heard the voice of Francis calling to him.

"Brother Leo," he said, "please bring the inkpot and your pen, for I wish to dictate something."

Leo hurried at once to obey. When he had crossed the bridge and was seated on a rock with the paper spread out before him, this is what Francis dictated:

"May the Lord bless you and keep you, Brother Leo! May He show His face to you, and have mercy on you. May He turn His countenance to you and give you peace. Brother Leo, may the Lord bless you!"

And then Francis, with a smile, signed it and told Leo to keep it always. Leo was happy again. He had not needed to ask. Francis had guessed his wish. He guarded the blessing all his life and it helped him through many dark days.

Not long after this the brothers were awakened one morning by a great light which was shining all about the cave of Francis. In great fear, Leo hurried across the bridge. There was Francis on his knees, as he had been praying all through the night. The great light shone down on his uplifted face and his arms were outstretched. He did not see Leo, but Leo at once saw that something very strange had happened to Francis. The palms of his hands showed the print of nails, and his feet had the same marks. Well did Leo know those marks. They were the same marks that our Lord had borne when He had been taken down from the cross. The Little Poor Man had become even more like the Master he had tried for so many years to imitate. For our Lord had signed him with His own wounds.

It was Friday, September fourteenth, of the year 1224 —the dawn of Holy Cross Day.

TWELVE

The Song at Sunset

ABOUT the Lady Clare's convent garden there hung the perfume of midsummer flowers holding their bright heads up to the blue Umbrian sky. The little shelter at the far end of the garden had a roof and walls, but no door. Francis could lie there on his bed of leaves and look out upon the garden, rejoicing in its beauty. He was very ill, but that did not keep him from being joyful.

"Did you know," he said one morning to Clare, who, with her nuns, came every day to take care of him, "that our sisters, the flowers, have their own language even as our sisters, the birds? As I lie here, I find it very pleasant to talk with them."

Francis had known the garden of old. Over there stood the stone bench on which long ago he used to sit with Father Julio. Just beyond the church, the olive tree to which he had once tied Raphael still spread its silvery green leaves. He knew that within the church the crucifix which had changed his whole life was hanging still above the altar. It was here that he had begun his work and he was happy in these memories. But he was suffering, also, because "Brother Jackass" was quite worn out from all the labors his master had made him perform.

"I apologize, Brother Jackass," said Francis one day. "It is no wonder that you hurt me, for certainly I have never treated *you* very well. But then, you see, we have had a great deal to do for our Lord and it isn't half finished yet." Francis sighed.

Just then the Lady Clare came in, bringing him a cool lemonade, and he began to feel better. She sat down beside him and soon he was smiling happily at all she had to relate. The Poor Ladies now had many new convents and sisters in other cities, and Clare was kept very busy. While Francis had been gone, the Lady Ortolana, now a widow, had come to join her two daughters in the convent of San Damiano. With her had come also Clare's youngest sister, Beatrix, and her aunt, Bianca. They, too, had given all they owned to the poor and now worked in the fields, or took care of the sick.

"My good friends, the Sciffi!" exclaimed Francis.

He was glad to hear that the gay Orlando had quieted down and become a worthy knight. His cousin, Brother Rufino, climbed the hill every day from the Little Portion to see Francis. And of course Leo and Angelo always came with him. All the friars made excuses to walk up to the convent garden, for they feared that Brother Francis would not long be with them.

Poor Juniper would try to hold back his tears by performing a *jongleur* dance. He never failed to make Francis laugh. Bernard, Giles, Illuminato, and Masseo all strove to cheer him with some good news about his order. Leo scarcely ever left his side. Francis was happy that now he had a great number of sons scattered far and wide, but he always said to those at his bedside:

"Remember to be faithful to the Lady Poverty!"

Then he would beg them to sing again the song of love he had composed in her honor. Each morning the sun came to awaken Francis and made him glad with its light and warmth. So now as he lay there, he composed another song to thank God for his good friend, the sun. He taught it to his friars and asked them to join him in singing it every day. When the music arose from the garden, Clare's nuns would run to the convent windows to hear the Hymn to the Sun:

"Praised be my Lord God, with all His creatures! Above all, with our Brother Sun, who brings us the day, and gives us the light. He is beautiful and radiant with great splendor!"

The people of Assisi were sad because Francis lay so

ill in the garden of San Damiano and the bishop, too, was greatly worried. When autumn came and the nights grew colder, he ordered the brothers to carry Francis to his own palace. There he could be warm and have every care. The friars came each day and gathered about the Little Poor Man, but he would not let them be sad.

"What!" he would exclaim. "All these long faces! Have I not always taught you to be joyful? Sing now, all of you, and lift up your hearts, for soon I am going to join my Lord!"

The brothers would sing at the top of their voices and Francis along with them. As Francis lay dying, they sang so much and made such a din in the palace that the poor bishop could not do his work and was forced to go away for a while.

At last one morning Francis said to his brothers:

"I think that Sister Death will come for me soon. I would like very much to meet her down at our own beloved Little Portion, so please carry me there."

They made a litter and carried him down to Saint Mary of the Angels. Not far from the city gates, and close to the house of his friends, the lepers, he asked the friars to set him down for a moment. Then, rising up, he looked for the last time upon his own city and made the sign of the cross over it and blessed it. It was the month of October, of the year 1226. Francis was only forty-four years old.

They laid him on a bed in the little house next to the

church of Saint Mary of the Angels, which he had repaired with his own hands. He would not leave the world without one final proof to the Lady Poverty that he was faithful to her until the end. He arose from the bed and took off his poor robe and cast it from him— just as on that day long ago he had laid all his fine clothing at the feet of his father. Then he lay down on the cold earth to die—the poorest of men, owning nothing.

He blessed all his sons who stood about him, and he blessed all those who were far away, and even those who would come after them, right down to our own day. It was to be a stretch of more than seven hundred years. The blessing continues for all those who follow the way of Francis and will continue until the end of time.

The sun was setting when Sister Death came to gather him up and carry him to his Lord. Then suddenly the sky over the Little Portion was filled with a great fluttering of wings. Hundreds of his friends, the larks, came flying to settle on the roof above him. And with their sweet song they sang their Brother Francis to sleep.

And After . . .

WITH one heart the people of Italy arose and demanded that Francis Bernardone be declared a saint. The Little Poor Man who had never thought himself worthy to become a priest became a saint before all the world in the summer of 1228, less than two years after his death. He lies in a beautiful church in Assisi which the brothers erected, and which is one of the wonders of the world.

The Lady Clare lived for many years after the death of Francis and, with her sisters, ever remained true to all that he had taught. Like Francis, she, too, had her experience with the Saracens.

War came to Italy and a great army set siege to Assisi. Its commander paid the Saracens to fight for him. One dark night they came rushing upon the convent of San Damiano with their fierce shouts and their cruel, curved swords. They would have killed Clare and her nuns; and then they would have gone on to the city to destroy it and murder all the people.

They were already climbing the walls of the convent when Clare, who was praying in the chapel, took up the Blessed Sacrament. Holding it high, she carried it to the window and, leaning far out, she held it before the shouting Saracens. At once their eyes were burned by a blinding light. They could not see; they stumbled and fell off the walls. And, in sheer terror, they ran away. After that, the commander could not get them to attack Assisi. All the people came out to thank the Lady Clare, for they knew that by her holy prayers she had saved them and their city.

Clare died in the summer of the year 1253. Two years later, she, too, was declared a saint. And today, among the birds and flowers of paradise, she stands right at the side of Francis.